Points

This is a work of fiction. Names, characters, places and incidents either are products of the author's imagination or used fictitiously and any resemblance to actual events or locales or persons, living or dead is entirely coincidental.

Cover Art by Hilary Rhodes www.hilaryrhodesdesign.com

POINTS

Library of Congress Control Number: 2020943852

Printed in the United States of America

ISBN 978-1-7339503-4-3 (Paperback Edition)
ISBN 978-1-7339503-5-0 (EPUB Edition)

Lang Verhaal Company
Chicago, Illinois
www.LangVerhaal.com

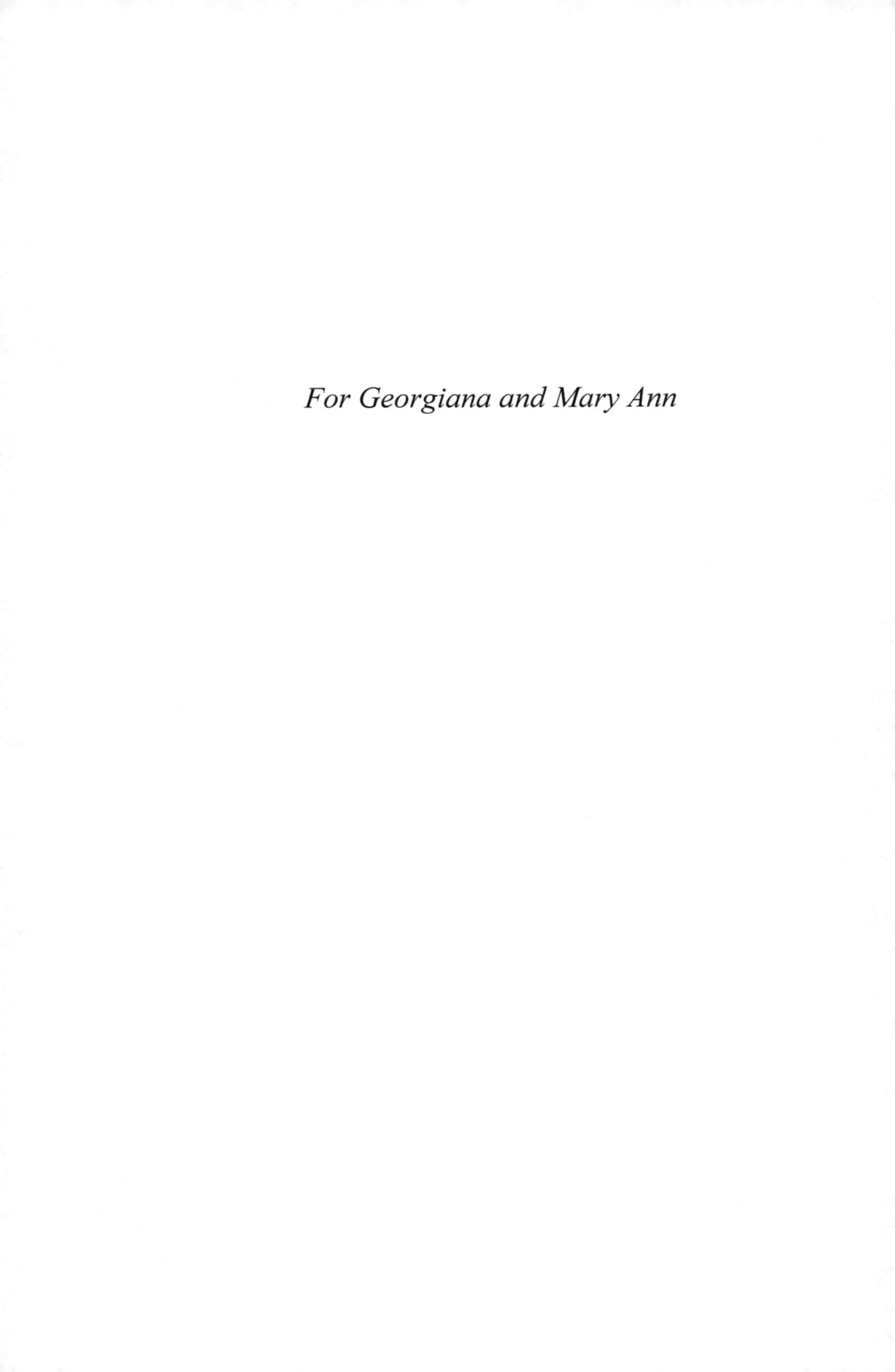

For Georgiana and Mary Ann

Points

By Lisa Doyle

Good girls go to heaven. Bad girls go everywhere.
~Helen Gurley Brown

PROLOGUE

"So, what should we do?"

I glanced at Ash. She was fiddling with the remnants of her burger wrapper, tearing away the corners and dropping them into her empty, grease-spattered container of fries. A napkin lay delicately underneath it across her lap, protecting her vintage, ice blue satin dress. Me, I didn't particularly care what I got on mine at this point. It was a waste, anyway.

"It's only ten after ten," she said dully. "Still about another hour until the dance ends. We should probably stay out another half hour so it's not …you know…suspect."

Instead of at the dance, we were sitting in the McDonald's parking lot, listening to Adele on repeat.

"I didn't mean tonight," I clarified. "I meant in the long run. What are we going to *do*?"

She bit her lip.

"Ugh," she replied. "I don't know, Bethany. Drop out?"

I gave her a long look. "That's a little extreme."

"Maybe we could transfer schools."

"Where to?"

"Um. Catholic school?"

"We're not Catholic."

"The guys might be a little nicer there at least," she offered.

"Doubtful," I scoffed.

"Homeschooling?"

"Have you *met* my mom? No."

"Hire a hitman?"

I snorted derisively. "Get serious, Ash."

"I don't see *you* coming up with any spectacular ideas," she huffed.

"Touché."

We were both quiet for a moment.

I leaned back in the driver's seat, closing my eyes, but before long I felt Ash, inches away from me, starting to gently shake.

"It's just so unfair," she said, her face crumpling. "What did we do? What are we doing so wrong? Why does this crap keep happening to us?" She fished around in the empty paper bag for a spare napkin and, not finding one, lightly dabbed at her eyes with the tip of her manicured pinky.

"I don't know, Ash," I mumbled. "Maybe it's because we *let* it happen to us. At least, I do."

Her face softened, knowing from what I'd told her, what Snow Ridge High School had been like for me until she had moved to town in August.

"Well," she said, reaching over and squeezing my hand. "Let's stop victim-shaming ourselves, okay?"

I gave her a wan smile back. "Okay."

Ash sniffed hard and shook her head, little, blonde curls waving like a willow tree. "And if anything," she added, "the idea about hiring a hitman is probably the best one. Just saying."

I managed a small laugh. "We could check Craigslist right now if you want."

She leaned back in her seat. "Course, my parents will be thrilled with this turn of events, anyway. They never liked him."

"Well. There's that," I woefully agreed. "Guess that gets rid of one problem."

"But leaves the rest of them. Because it's systemic, you know."

We both fell silent.

After a moment I heard Ash *hmmm.*

"What?"

"I was just thinking about something my old pastor said years ago. Before I ever moved to Germany."

"What was that?"

"'When you see a problem, you're anointed to solve it.'"

I rolled my eyes. "Is that right," I said, balling up my napkin and shoving it into the bottom of my bag.

Ash turned and looked at me, eyes gleaming bright.

"Just hear me out."

CHAPTER 1
FOUR MONTHS EARLIER

My mom couldn't stop ugly crying. Loudly. The other people in line were starting to stare.

"It's just *so far away*," she said, sniffling and wiping her eyes with the back of her hand.

Not far enough in my opinion.

"I know, I know, Mom," Christian said, drawing her in for a hug. "But the six months are gonna fly right by. I promise."

"Well, we're really proud of you," Dad added, reaching out his arm and resting it on Christian's shoulder. "It's not every kid who'd make an amazing choice like this."

I snorted. My parents both glared at me, but I said nothing, and pretended to be fascinated by the massive list of Departures twinkling above my head. The "amazing choice" Dad was referring to was my brother Christian's answer to a gap year: a six-month stint volunteering to build homes for Habitat for Humanity. On the Gold Coast of Australia. About fifty feet from the beach.

And the reason *why* he was suddenly such a philanthropist? Well, that's because his full-ride soccer scholarship to North Central College had disappeared when he tore his ACL in June. It would be one thing if it had been a tragic injury caused during a game-winning goal, or if he'd fallen victim to a cheap shot by an opponent. But it's quite another when you end your own athletic career because you were drunk at Kylie Stevenson's graduation party, and someone bet you $20 that you were too scared to jump off the second-story roof while screaming "Class of 2018 rules!"

My parents had been upset that he'd lost the scholarship but were infinitely more grateful that he was alive. I was initially shocked that he could have been so flipping (literally) stupid and irresponsible, and that my parents couldn't see that; then, I reminded myself that this was how it's always been. For as long as I could remember, Christian could do no wrong in their eyes, and that was that.

And, that was the general MO in Snow Ridge, Illinois, the far western suburb of Chicago where we lived (est. 1868). My family was in its fourth generation here, which, believe it or not, is on the lower end of the average in this town. It's a cherry-red community anchored into a bright blue state, complete with brick streets in its picturesque downtown, and it certainly earned the nickname that's snickered at all our away games: So Rich.

There was a very certain way of life here, and pretty much everyone followed it. Dads worked; moms didn't. This was also true in my family. My dad ran his independent State Farm agency (Cummings Insurance, est. 1966) passed to him when Grandpa died, and as far as I could tell, his job primarily involved ample amounts of golf, racquetball, and lunch with his high school buddies. Mom spent most of her days being a sports mom/personal assistant to Christian. And I spent most of my time trying to keep out of the way.

I wish I could say I was with my friends instead, but no—I wasn't exactly overflowing with them. Thing is, I never understood the way girls operated in Snow Ridge. Well, rather, it wasn't *how* they operated that I couldn't piece together—I just didn't understand *why*.

Here's just an example. On the first day of second grade, the boys in my class all decided they were going to play kickball at recess, right? And they were real jerks to the girls in my class about it, sneering that "girls suck at sports" and they weren't allowed to play with them. (Never mind the fact that the teachers and lunch monitors didn't say one word about this.) And the girls, instead of playing their own game of kickball—or even drawing with chalk, playing hopscotch, or whatever—one by one, they made their way over to the sidelines to "play cheerleader" for the boys and spent recess making up cheers and dances in their honor. Even at seven, I knew this was weird. But no one else did, so I just side-eyed the situation and doodled in my journal.

True, I was never bullied per se. That wasn't the Snow Ridge way because everyone knew each other in Snow Ridge; in fact, their grandparents, even *grandparents' grandparents* in some cases, knew each other. This meant I was included in birthday parties and sleepovers and stuff by default, since my parents were golf buddies with their parents. Didn't mean I belonged, though. I was always at the edge of the lunch table, in the farthest sleeping bag from the center, and destined for the torn valentine from the variety pack. Basically, I was the bag of Smarties at the bottom of the trick-or-treat bag: still acceptable, but barely.

Though, the big positive of this was that as I got older, I found myself preferring to be alone more often than not and embarked on my lifelong love affair with books. And as any true bibliophile knows, these books often became replacements for friends. Let's be honest, I liked the characters in them better than I liked the people around me. I'd devoured every book in *The Babysitters' Club* series and imagined myself as Mary Ann while totally shipping Claudia's style. I've always felt like I was in the wrong story in my real life. Why wouldn't I just go to my shelf anytime I wanted and imagine myself in a different one?

Plus, there was always something to do when I was on the bleachers, dragged to all of Christian's soccer crap nine weekends out of ten, as it was clear early on that I sure as heck wasn't going to be anywhere on the field. My parents chided me to "pay attention to the game" and "be supportive," but I say they were lucky I got out of the car at all.

Anyway, back to Australia's new savior, Christian. He'd visibly been in pain from the surgery and physical therapy this past summer, but that wasn't what got him down. He was mostly depressed about two things: his soccer career ending and having to go off to his freshman year in college and witness a season operating without him. He'd never admit it, but he was definitely nervous about starting college without the athlete badge of honor—he'd be just another freshman. And he'd never been just another anything in his life. Hence, his idea to move to another hemisphere; party on the beach all fall and winter; sleep with a bunch of tan Aussie blondes unfamiliar with his player reputation; and somehow look like a do-gooder in the process. Christian was killing a whole flock of birds with this one stone.

"Well, before you know it, you'll be home before March and ready for the spring quarter," Mom said, trying to buck up.

She pulled a tissue from her purse and dabbed at her eyes. Christian put his arm around her, and she rested her head against his shoulder.

Honestly, *they* looked like siblings more than he and I did, with their matching dark blonde hair, perfectly tanned skin and Atlantic-blue eyes. They even were both wearing polos and khakis today. I favored my dad more in looks, with dark brown hair and eyes, but it's anyone guess why I'm not like any of them on the inside. I think the three of them read two books a year, combined. To be fair, that's the same amount of soccer games I'll watch annually now, and that's with a lot of arm twisting.

"Sure you don't want to apply for citizenship while you're down there?" I asked innocently.

"You wish," he said with a smirk.

I did wish, in fact. I'd be perfectly happy if he stayed halfway around the world forever, though I knew it wasn't likely. Truth be told, I felt a little badly for how college was going to unfurl for him—but not *that* badly. I certainly had spent a good sixteen years living the "not anyone special" dream.

Trust me, having an older brother that everyone drools over is not.that.great. Especially when you get to high school and, except for a three-week stint your freshman year, you're completely invisible. And let's just see here—did Christian, Mr. Homecoming Court, three-sport athlete, and voted "Most Likely to be *The Bachelor*," ever once try to help me out? Invite me to a single party? Did he even say hi when he passed me in the hallway? Did he ever make an effort to bring me out of anonymity?

Hell no! He barely acknowledged me at home, let alone at school. Ever. I was a total disappointment to him and always had been. You take away our shared DNA and I don't think we had anything in common. So what was the point in pretending otherwise?

We inched up closer to the front of the line, and finally we reached the desk. Christian lugged his suitcase and frame backpack onto the counter and completed his dealings with the airline's check-in employee by himself while my parents looked on in unabashed pride.

"Guess this is where I take off," he said, as we hovered by security.

Mom hugged him like her life depended on it and resumed her crying, and even Dad looked like he had some dust in his eye. I checked my watch. Hopefully we'd get home in time for *Married at First Sight.*

"Bye," I said flatly. He nodded to me in return, then passed through the gate. Not to see Snow Ridge for the next six months.

God, I wished that could be me.

CHAPTER 2

My junior year started just a few days later. I wasn't expecting much to be different, and the first day was basically like any other first day had been. Keeping my head down and taking notes in class. Trying to ignore people as they avoided eye contact right back. Counting down the minutes until I could get home and away from the constant din of people I didn't care about and who cared nothing for me.

Until Spanish class.

As the first person to walk into my Spanish classroom that day, I grabbed a prime seat by the window air conditioner unit (because God forbid they install central air in a historic Snow Ridge building). I stood in front of the unit, fanning the sweat off my back rapidly with my shirt, eyes closed and basking in the privacy…when I heard his voice.

"Bethany? That you?"

I froze and then opened my eyes.

Oh my God.

It was none other than Harrison Dorsey. Now let me tell you, he'd changed since the last time I'd seen him in the flesh four years ago—and in that time he went from cereal-box-kid adorable to drop dead *gorgeous*.

Standing in the doorway across the room, I had the full view of him. He'd shot up to well over six feet tall, with the long, muscular build of an Olympian, plus a shock of auburn hair and a spattering of freckles across his face. When we were in middle school, I secretly thought of him as "Prince Harry." Hey, the shoe fit back then—and now, more so than ever.

I wouldn't say we were close when we were kids, but I did know him well enough to tell that he was different from the other boys. He was better. Once, on Field Day, he let me tag him out in dodgeball, knowing I was probably the worst athlete in the school. And I kid you not, he smiled and *winked* at me as he jogged to the sideline. I'd been living off that wink for a good four years.

He was a year older than me, and not long after that fateful Field Day, he shipped out to a boarding school near Wisconsin—recruited for their lacrosse club, and yes, that was a thing for eighth graders apparently. But, he didn't cut ties to Snow Ridge despite that. In fact, I heard he was dating Mara Frost, who'd graduated alongside Christian.

"Harrison, right?" I said, looking probably as red as I felt on the inside. "You, um, go here now?"

"Yeah," he said, ambling over to me and plopping himself in the seat next to mine. I nearly swooned. "Coach Richie recruited me back here for senior lacrosse."

"Wow," I said. "Um. That's cool."

Seriously, Bethany, that's all you can think of to say? I silently chided myself.

"Well," he said, with a grin. "It's good to see a friendly face. What've you been up to the last few years?"

I tried to hide my shock. What would I even say? Umm, completing Goodreads challenges and binging on bad reality TV?

Of course, it was a totally honest question. He wouldn't have asked had he known.

See, the summer I started high school, I had, um "blossomed." I'd been a scrawny kid, but in the span of the three months between eighth grade graduation and freshman year, I grew about five inches taller, could successfully fill out a C cup, and my body looked way more Fifth Harmony than fifth grader.

Guys noticed this.

I was asked to Homecoming by Shane McAdams (of McAdams Masonry, Est. 1897), a sophomore on the football team. Three weeks before the dance, he'd come up to my locker with a massive poster board, reading, "*Bethany, will you go to Homecoming with me?*" and two boxes underneath for me to either check "Yes" or "No." He handed me an equally massive magic marker, and blushing, I checked "Yes."

Frankly, I was surprised that Shane looked at me as anything other than Christian Cummings' mousy little sister, let alone that he would feel compelled to ask me to a dance in a super-elaborate, public way. But he seemed like a nice enough guy, and, moreover, cute. We flirted in the hallways, and he even saved me a seat at his lunch table.

I couldn't believe it. People were talking to me and *interested* in what I had to say. Not just guys, but girls, too—the same ones whose eyes for years had flitted past me like I wasn't there—were suddenly chatting me up in the hallway, hugging me when we passed each other between classes, asking to partner up with me in Bio. It was like I'd vaulted to the upper level of the Snow Ridge social strata without even trying.

Until the actual night of the dance.

I'd felt amazing before I left the house—my mom had taken me to Nordstrom, and I'd selected a short, electric blue number with cutout sides. Mom curled my hair and did my makeup, and for the first time, I knew what it was like to think, *Damn, I look good.*

Shane apparently agreed. He'd spent most of the evening staring at my boobs and sneaking sips of vodka in a poorly-concealed flask. Every time we slow danced, he kept pulling me way too close. Like, "definitely notice the pocket rocket" level of close, inching his hand up my thigh and under my dress on the dance floor. He wasn't even trying to be discreet about it, either. Like, we were inches away from all his football buddies and their dates, and he'd still continue to grope me, right there in the fieldhouse.

I remember him kissing my neck, the hot breath and Popov scent making my stomach turn, but I'd felt almost frozen on the inside and just kept dancing, thinking, *Well, this must be what they do in high school, right?* After driving me home, he'd tried to kiss me on my doorstep at the end of the night, his slobbery tongue coming at me like a creature from the deep. I'd whipped my head to the side so fast that he only violated my earlobe.

Shane creeped me out on a minor level, but not having anything else to compare it to, I kind of chalked it up to just a weird first-ever date. After all, aren't your teen years supposed to be the time of awkward first kisses and whatnot? Though, what I didn't anticipate was the fact that I quickly became a total social reject after Homecoming.

Not only did Shane throw looks of contempt my way every time he saw me (like seriously, what was I guilty of?), so did all his friends. And then so did basically every guy in this school. And, just as quickly, the connections I had to the girls quickly frayed, too.

Two years later, and I still didn't know exactly what Shane told people about me. But it couldn't have been good.

I tried to hold on to my newfound girlfriends the best I could, but there's only so many unanswered texts I could send before the shame of my desperation stopped me from sending any more. Besides, it became clear so quickly that the cliques in my high school were just as defined and tightened as they'd been in middle—and without Shane being adjacent, there wasn't a spot for me in any of them. Before I knew it, I was on my own. And unlike before—back when I hadn't ever tasted popularity—it wasn't by choice.

But Harrison probably didn't know about any of that. Thank God.

"You know, this and that," I cooed offhandedly.

He grinned. "Well I'll have to get to the bottom of it sometime."

Oh, the double entendres I could make outta that…

I'd barely noticed, but the classroom had filled up around us. Our teacher, Sr. Applebaum, ambled in, looking a little worse for the wear, with his shirt only half tucked into his khakis and smelling suspiciously like last night's happy hour. (#tenured #outofeffstogive)

"Vamonos, clase," Sr. Applebaum had drawled in the least Spanish accent known to humankind. "Pagina…uh, cinco."

We all dutifully opened our textbooks…to the copyright page.

Harrison leaned over to me and whispered, "How do you say 'functional alcoholic' in Spanish?"

I blushed.

"Um," I replied under my breath. "Are you sure about 'functional?'"

He let out a belly laugh, and Sr. Applebaum shot him a dirty look. Harrison quickly turned the laugh into a cough.

And just like that, Spanish became my bright spot of the day.

Not two hours later, I was sitting at my café-sized lunch table, alone and reading ahead for English Lit, when I noticed a commotion at the adjacent table. I saw Lindsay, always excited by new toys, dragging a blonde girl I didn't recognize to her lunch table.

Some of my earliest memories are of playdates with Lindsay. No, it's not that we were besties since kindergarten, but she ditched me when we got to high school. It's because our *moms* have been besties since kindergarten. They used to congratulate themselves on their "perfect planning," with Christian being slightly older than Lindsay and me being her same age, so that in their ideal world, those two would get married and I'd be the best friend/maid of honor/godmother to future children. No. Really. Our moms talked about this all the time. Wasn't anywhere close to reality, though, with me in the picture.

Lindsay is everything I'm not: Disney Channel-pretty. Outgoing. Confident. Blonde (surprise). To her credit, she's never been outright mean or vicious toward me. But like Christian, she wasn't interested in being friends with me, either. Even as a toddler you know when you're not in the same league as someone.

But Christian and Lindsay were two peas in a pod, so they would usually pair up and ditch me. They'd go to the far end of the playground and leave me on the swing, desperately kicking my legs and trying to go higher alone. But I never could.

Anyway, Lindsay plopped herself smack in the middle of the table, yanking the new girl there with her, and the rest of the table pounced like kittens on a mouse:

"So you're from Germany? What languages do you speak?"

"German, French, some Italian. And English."

"Not Spanish? I would think you'd have to know Spanish. You practically have to know it here, anyway."

"Um. I guess."

"So what does your dad do that made you guys have to move over there?"

"He works for Bosch."

"Ooh, is he like the president? Did they send him back to run the American division or what? You guys must be doing *well*, right?"

The new girl physically recoiled, then collected herself. "He asked to be transferred back. I mean, my Mom, my brothers and me, we're all American. We lived in Elmhurst until fourth grade."

"Oh…I thought you were *German*-German."

"Just half. Sorry to disappoint you," the girl said, looking not sorry at all.

The conversation quickly shifted back to Lindsay's latest first-world problem of the day (no, really: each day, she announced Lindsay's First-World Problem of the day, ranging from her step tracker dying before she could recharge it, to a snag in her thumbnail and being without an emery board), and the new girl looked around, taking in her surroundings. She caught my eye and looked at me warily, silently asking, *Is this chick for real?*

I looked back at her and silently responded with my eyebrows, *Yep. Welcome to Snow Ridge High School.*

As the week went on, Lindsay continued to cheerfully bring the new girl to the table, and people continued to ask her about Germany and compare notes with her on their own European travels. But each new day arrived at lunch, people scooted in, not out for her to sit. And, within a week, there was no spot left for her at all.

"Sorreeee," Lindsay said, shrugging with her hands up, like that purple-shirted emoji.

"Don't be," the new girl said, flashing a knowing smirk.

The new girl glanced at me, smiled when she caught my eye, and sat down without the slightest trace of disappointment.

"This seat taken?" she asked brightly.

"Go ahead," I said, moving my backpack off the table.

"I'm Ash Bauer."

"Bethany Cummings."

Again, she smiled at me and pulled her bento box from her backpack. As she assembled the various parts of her lunch—a wrap, carrots, yogurt and a large peanut butter brownie—I noticed a copper bangle with delicate cursive etching on her wrist.

"I love your bracelet," I said, pointing at it. "What's it say?"

"*Was mich nicht umbringt, macht mich starker*," she replied in perfectly clipped German. "Or in English, 'what doesn't kill you makes you stronger.'"

"True enough," I agreed, taking a generous bite of my turkey sandwich.

"My dad got it for me, just before we moved back here," she added.

"Well," I muttered, "Sounds like you at least got some advance warning." I then immediately clamped my hand over my mouth. *Shoot*, I thought, *why'd I just say that?*

She raised an eyebrow and then snickered. "Now, *you* I'm gonna like," she said, then took a large bite of her brownie first.

CHAPTER 3

Don't get me wrong. Snow Ridge, on the whole, still royally sucked. But it was a little bit more manageable now that I had Ash.

Ash had a distinctively European look about her that went beyond her almost white-blonde hair, blue eyes and unblemished skin. She was pretty—*very* pretty, in fact, not a rarity in Snow Ridge. The difference was that she didn't let her natural gorgessity affect her attitude. She didn't have an ounce of entitlement in her nor a mean bone in her body. Ash also had a sense of maturity, an air about her that made her seem older than sixteen. Plus, she was kind of quiet on the outside, like me.

Maybe it was her German upbringing, but Ash had a really logical, matter-of-fact way of looking at things, and was always looking for the most efficient way to do anything. Whether it was a shortcut to save her 30 seconds of driving time or her impressive ability to calculate sales tax in her head before arriving at the register, exact change in hand, Ash had no time for nonsense. She wasn't cold at all though, and anyone who spent five minutes with her knew that.

Ash and I just clicked, and we had the kind of friendship where we could say the weirdest or most brutally honest things to each other without worrying about being judged. And after sixteen years of silence on my thoughts about Snow Ridge and the people living here, I had *plenty* to say.

It was more obvious to me than it might have been to most people, but Snow Ridge girls didn't like Ash much. They treated her like a novelty at first, but when she didn't go along with their prissy attitudes, she got dropped pretty quickly. Then, since she was clearly tight with me, she really wasn't gonna have much of a shot of becoming queen bee (not like she cared). But finally, the straw that really shattered the camel's back beyond surgical repair was Dane Alexander.

Let me back up. Ash hadn't been allowed to date when she was in Germany. That was one of her ultra-conservative mom's rules when moving to liberal Europe, and as far as her mom knew, Ash was still as pure as the driven snow.

Ash had confided to me that she'd actually dated three guys while living in Stuttgart—all of them at least two years older than her, all of them good-looking, all of them secret. And, pragmatic as ever, all of them she considered a learning experience.

"Sure, every breakup sucked in its own way, but I don't regret dating any of them," she explained to me. "You move on. You figure out what you want from the next guy. Hakuna matata and all that."

I seriously envied her ability to shake it off. Back then, anyway.

When her family moved to Snow Ridge, her parents had told her they'd relax the "no-dating" rule as they were less worried about the golden Snow Ridge boys violating their daughter. After all, this town had more churches per capita than almost any other town in the area and was as well known for its strong community values as it was for its football team.

What Mrs. Bauer didn't take into account was the blatant boys club in this town and the sheer attitude that legit every guy in this town had, like they'd entered a competition and won before the game even started. Sorry to break it to you, Snow Ridge parents, but despite any etched-in-stone, centuries-old reputation this town may have, it doesn't account for anyone's actions. And no matter how many PTA workshops you attend or how many blogs you read about how to raise your kids right, at some point…well, if your kid's truly a big, fat jerk, then he (or she) is going to behave like a big, fat jerk. And what was it they said about apples falling from trees, and chips and blocks…?

The Snow Ridge guys were after Ash from day one. But, when she didn't respond right away to them with the flirtatious grins or squeals of, "Oh, *stahp!*" like they were used to, most of them didn't try much harder. But, for some guys that just meant the thrill of the chase was that much sweeter—and for Dane Alexander, that was the case.

Dane Alexander (Alexander Elementary School, est. 1954) was senior class president that year. Hot in a Ken doll way, if you're into Ken dolls, with wavy brown hair, dimples and a trillion-watt smile. Everyone without a Y chromosome (and some with one) nursed a crush on him of varying degrees—well, pretty much everyone, except for Ash, because she didn't particularly give a crap or see why she should.

But, one day in early September, Ash and I had sat down to lunch at the edge of our table, as usual, when we heard a voice say, "Excuse me?"

We looked up, and Dane Alexander was standing there in his button-down and chinos, next to a sullen-looking Lindsay.

She cleared her throat, and I swear it physically pained her to say, "Dane. I'd like you to meet my—" she paused and gave the slightest shudder, "*friend*, Ash Bauer."

That was news to us.

Ash looked blankly at him.

"Hi?" she said.

He grinned at her.

"How do you do?" he said, charm oozing out of his pores. "I'd heard we had a new European transplant, but I didn't know you'd be so lovely." Oh, geez, eye roll.

Ash actually blushed a small amount. I stole a glance at Lindsay, and if looks could kill, she'd have been locked up for life.

"Mind if I join you?" Dane asked, still smiling.

"Um, maybe some other time," Ash said. "I have to finish off my Trig homework before class next period."

"Yes, no need to bother the poor girl," Lindsay said clipping the end of each word. "I'll see you at peer jury, Dane," she added, sauntering back over to her table.

"Bye now," he said to Ash with a wink, completely ignoring Lindsay.

Thus started him visiting our lunch table every day. He was unfailingly polite, even chatted with me a bit, but he was clearly there to get to know Ash. Little by little, she opened up to him, and even began saving him a seat.

After about three weeks of this, he finally did what I could see coming from a mile away (though Ash swears she hadn't): he asked her to Homecoming. Complete with a glee club flash mob performing "You're the One That I Want," from *Grease*, and Dane leading the way, dressed like Danny Zuko.

"Ash B, will you be my Sandra Dee, and go to Homecoming with me?" he'd asked at the end of the performance, down on one knee in front of her, brow glistening with sweat.

Ash turned about fifty shades of red and nodded.

"Yes," she said, laughing. "Now get up."

I cheered and hooted for them, along with all the other tables full of people who'd turned around to see. Except, everyone at the table adjacent to us, because they golf-clapped with small pinched smiles. Though, Lindsay couldn't even join in for that much. No, even Lindsay couldn't hide an internal scream face like *that*.

Anyway, Dane took Ash not only to Homecoming, but also to a huge post-Homecoming weekend at his parents' summer home in New Buffalo ("supervised" by his parents, allegedly). I followed all of Ash's pics and stories that she posted, and it looked like the whole weekend was perfect. As soon as Ash got back into town, I came over to help unpack and grill her for all the details.

I could tell she was hiding something; her smile was strained while we were downstairs and around her family. As soon as we were up in her room, though, we situated ourselves on her bed and she broke it all down.

"Everything was good the first day. We played beach volleyball, grilled burgers and steaks, and then the campfire at night where we roasted s'mores. It was like straight out of a Ralph Lauren commercial. But then…it all went to hell."

"What happened?" I asked softly.

"Ugh," she said, fighting back tears and pulling her knees up to her chest. "It got cold out, so I went up to the girl's bedroom to grab my hoodie. So I'm digging through my bag, looking around, and I hear a guy's voice behind me."

"Was it Dane?"

"No, it was Seamus Dean. Standing in the doorway."

Ugh was right. Seamus was the son of the dean of Snow Ridge High. (Yes, everyone saw the irony, and often referred to his dad as Dean Squared.) If I thought Christian's problem with acting entitled was bad—which I did think—Seamus's problem was about six times worse. For Halloween one year, he came to school dressed up in a cardboard box wrapped like a present, and the tag read "From God, To Women." The license plate on his bright orange Wrangler read "NO SEAM."

But what was really suspicious? Seamus had been out of school all year—nearly two months so far—and no one knew where he'd been. Or, if people knew, they weren't saying.

"Oh, Christ," I said, rolling my eyes. "Was this the first time you met him?"

"Yeah. He kept joking about being sprung from prison. Was he joking?"

There wasn't any humor in her eyes.

"Honestly, I wouldn't be shocked. He's the worst," I admitted. "What'd he say to you?"

"It's not what he said. It's what he *did*," she said quietly

I grew cold. Ash looked at me mournfully, then continued.

"I was all, 'Hey, Seamus,' and was about to put my sweatshirt on. And he was all, 'You sure you need that extra layer?' And I'm like, 'Yeah, it's pretty chilly out there.' And then he was like, 'Well, why don't we just stay inside for a bit? I'm a really good cuddler, I'll warm you right up.'"

"Seriously?" I said, grimacing.

"Yeah. And I tried to be all 'Oh, haha,' because what else am I supposed to do? And I smile and then try to walk past him, and then he holds up an arm so he's blocking the doorway."

My stomach started to drop.

Ash continued. "So again, I was like, 'Haha, very funny, Seamus. Let me pass.' But he wouldn't. So I'm trying to keep it light and try to plow through his arm, and then he wraps his arms around me in this big, creepy-ass bear hug. And the next thing I know he's *sucking on my neck.*"

"What the hell?"

"And I go, 'Cut that out, Seamus!' And totally elbow him in the gut. He lets go and gets this—this *look* in his eyes and smacks me *hard* on the ass on the way out of the room. I looked the next morning, and it left an actual bruise."

"Again, *what the hell*," I said, shaking my head. "Did you tell anybody?"

"Well, yeah," she said, now her tears spilling over. "I told Dane, but I waited until the next morning when he was driving us back from Michigan. I didn't want things to get weird for everyone else there that night, you know."

Two months in Snow Ridge, and already Ash's concern wasn't that she'd been sexually assaulted—it was about making his friends feel awkward about it.

Unfortunately, I understood.

"Sure," I said, nodding and rubbing her back. "How did he react?"

"He didn't believe me." She blew her nose.

"He thought you were making it up?"

"Well, no. Not exactly," she said. "I told him, and he was like, 'I'm sure you're overreacting. Seamus was probably just kidding around. Plus, he was drunk.'"

"That's all he had to say?"

"Basically. I told him I was still really pissed about it and he was like, 'Well, it'll blow over. I'll talk to Seamus.' And then he just turned the music up and started singing along for the rest of the ride home."

"This is total crap, Ash," I said, shaking my head.

"I know," she said, flopping backward on the bed and rubbing her temples. "I really don't know how I can feel any worse right now."

I had no idea how much worse either until I walked into the commons the next day. I went to the vending machine to get a coffee, and I saw written in a Sharpie on the wall right behind it, "Ash Bauer is a ho."

I started to shake. *What?*

A senior I vaguely knew from my gym class, Emma, had wandered into line next to me just then.

She must have seen the look on my face because she eyed me warily and said, "You okay, Bethany?"

I took a deep breath and figured I might as well ask.

"Um," I said, nodding toward the graffiti. "You know anything about that? Like why, who…?"

She read it and her eyes widened, then flashed with recognition.

"Oh," she said. "Yeah. I heard she blew like four different guys at post-prom at Dane Alexander's lake house. None of them Dane Alexander."

"What?" I hissed. "That's a complete and total lie."

Emma shrugged. "That's what people've been saying."

I stumbled away without even getting my coffee, weighted down with the anvil of this rumor. As much as it would hurt her, Ash had to know—and I knew it would be better in the long run if she heard it from me.

I waited at the foot of the stairwell I knew she'd take on her way down to lunch and pulled her aside.

"What's going on?" she'd asked, brow furrowing as she saw how distressed I was.

"There's something you have to hear," I said carefully. "Just don't shoot the messenger."

I'll never forget the way Ash's face looked when I told her: seeing her flash with anger at the falseness of the rumor; watching her crumple in sadness at the utter humiliation, knowing that no matter what she did to defend herself, the rumor was out there, and over two thousand Snow Ridgians would believe what they wanted. Because, really, who would be there for Ash to prove otherwise?

But the worst part of it was seeing something visibly break inside Ash. The strength she'd had, the *c'est la vie* attitude she'd had about love, it was like they'd had a heart attack and died on the spot. And it left her changed forever.

Just as she'd started to cry, I pulled her in for a hug, holding her tight. When I opened my eyes, I saw Seamus sashay by on his way into the commons. His eye caught mine, and I know for a fact I saw a gleam in them before he diverted them and sauntered into the boys' bathroom. I also saw a Sharpie clutched in his smug, meaty hand.

There was no way to *prove* he had started the rumor. But that doesn't mean he didn't do it.

CHAPTER 4

You'd think this might have turned us off from guys altogether. Or at least kept us from being gluttons for punishment.

Nope.

Ash, with what was left of her plummeting self-esteem, was subconsciously looking for the opposite of Dane, and soon started hanging out with Matt Greengrass. He was a fifth-year senior who wore cargo shorts and too much gel in his hair for my taste, plus he smoked like a chimney. His claim to fame was getting banned from pep rallies when he'd started a small-to-medium sized fire from the balcony his senior year (excuse me, his *first* senior year).

You get the picture.

And me? Every day, I found myself falling more and more in love with Harrison.

We automatically paired up for every partner exercise. Harrison always looked amazing—that was a given—and I felt butterflies every time I saw him come into the Spanish classroom, which settled slightly every time he sat next to me and greeted me with his ever-present grin. And he was a really well-liked guy—bro-hugs and handshakes with guys left and right, and all the girls noticed him, whether they tried to hide it or not. I'd heard he and Mara were playing things by ear and weren't totally over or totally not over per se. But the way he paid attention to me and acted like I was the only girl in the room for those 48 minutes each day? I *lived* for that.

It was one day right before Halloween, and Harrison came into class totally subdued—not like him at all. Of course, I immediately worried he was mad at me or something and spent the next 15 minutes with a stomachache over it.

When we partnered up to work on the past conjugative tense, I whispered, "Que pasó?"

He looked at me, sadder than I'd ever seen him before. In fact, Harrison was never sad—not that I'd ever seen.

He whispered back, "Mara dumped me. Said the long-distance thing was too hard with her up at Madison."

Really?

Stay calm, stay calm, stay calm, I thought.

Poor guy. He looked so miserable, like his dog had just died or something, that I almost felt bad from feeling so gleeful about it. Don't get me wrong; I wanted to make it better for Harrison. I wanted to wrap him in my arms, kiss him, make him forget all about Mara. I wanted him to open his eyes, look at me *in that way.*

I wanted what was impossible.

"Lo siento," I said, frowning in sympathy. He looked back at me with puppydog eyes.

Screw it, I'm going for it, I decided.

I reached over and gave his hand a squeeze, too.

Oh my God. He squeezed back.

But I didn't get any other signs from him for weeks after that. We were still friends for sure, but I'd had to admit to myself that this crush was definitely one-sided.

So I could barely contain my excitement when, about two weeks later, he asked me—specifically and to my face!—if I wanted to go to a party at Hugh Treeger's, from the lacrosse team.

"Definitely!" I said, then immediately regretted coming on so strong.

But he didn't flinch. And I was going to my first party since…good God, in years.

That was the last thing he said to me about the party that week, though. And I wasn't about to hound Harrison for pertinent details, like if he would give me a ride, or what time the party was supposed to start. No, that kind of thing would make me look desperate, and he didn't offer them up.

Ash had already planned on hanging out at Matt's that night (with me as an alibi). So I borrowed my mom's Buick and drove myself to Hugh's around 8, pulling up to a sprawling, palatial house in Snow Ridge Estates, where the *really* So Rich people lived. To give you an idea, I passed several manses with stables and horse fields along the way to his cul-de-sac.

I wore a moto jacket over my cutest white top, possibly a little too see-through for my own good, and my shortest navy skirt to go with it. Well, if I was going to flaunt it, might as well in the presence of a guy I was into, right?

I parked at the far end of the driveway and walked up the gravel driveway to the house. I rang the doorbell and waited anxiously outside, hearing the music thumping away. About a minute later, the door swung open, and I was facing Hugh, who was holding a plastic red cup and sporting a drunken grin. He had the same rangy lacrosse player build as Harrison: thick brown hair, stubble, some acne and remnants of a sunburn. He was wearing a lifeguard shirt for the Snow Ridge Estates Country Club.

"Hi. Um. Harrison Dorsey invited me?" I squeaked.

Hugh gave me the once over, and then the twice over, which had me slightly unnerved. Just being near him had me feeling like I was alone in a parking garage.

"Did he now," he drawled.

My heart was in my stomach. This was a mistake.

And just then, a barefoot Harrison walked by, his face breaking into a grin.

"You made it!" he said. And before I knew it, he was next to me, an arm slung casually over my shoulder (!) and said to Hugh, "This is Bethany Cummings."

"Hi," I said, feeling electrified from the sensation of his arm on me.

Hugh raised an eyebrow at me.

"You Christian's sister?"

Sigh.

"Yep," I replied.

"And, he's in Australia now, right?"

"Yep."

Hugh slowly grinned. "C'mon in."

And so we did, Harrison's arm falling off me (boo) as we stepped up into the house. Hugh led us to the massive sunken family room where there were about a dozen people. Some were engaged in a game of beer pong, and a group of girls from the swim team were chatting in the corner and nursing bottles of Lagunitas.

Hugh pulled open the door to the mini fridge and pulled out a six pack of Bud Light.

"You guys got here just in time for Power Hour," he said. "Wanna play?"

I hesitated. What the heck was Power Hour?

Sensing my unasked question, Harrison said, "That's where you take a shot of beer every minute for an hour, right?"

"Yeah," Hugh said, extricating handfuls of shot glasses from behind the bar. "You guys in?"

He handed us each a shot glass before receiving an answer.

I took a deep breath. "Sounds good," I said. Never mind the fact that I'd only had a few sips of beer here and there before. But a shot wasn't all that much for beer, right? Especially if it was light.

Half an hour later, I had proven myself entirely wrong. I excused myself from the game halfway through and made it to the bathroom to break the seal, feeling woozy. I stumbled back toward the den. Before I turned the corner to go in, I heard Hugh's gravelly voice.

"What's the deal with you and that girl you brought?" he said.

"Bethany?" Harrison replied.

My heart skipped a beat at hearing him say my name.

"She's cool, I guess," Harrison continued. "She's just a friend."

Just a friend. What a knife through the heart. Just when I thought that maybe he was returning some of the many feelings I had for him, just when I thought our friendship could become something more, just when he'd put his arm around me—none of it meant anything. Not to him, anyway. I don't think I'd ever felt so deflated in all my life.

"Oh, okay," Hugh said. "Just wondering.

"Why?"

"She's half-cute."

Huh, I thought, my mind still a little fuzzy. Maybe Hugh could…I could….

So, about half an hour later, with my head still swimming and my limbs still loose, Hugh asked me to go the back deck to look at the stars with him. And I agreed. And when he kissed me, I let him. And when he started to move his hand under my shirt, I stiffened for just a moment. But then I let him do that, too. It's true, I didn't say no. And I wiped the tears from the corner of my eyes before he could notice them.

CHAPTER 5

That's all that happened with me and Hugh that night. No need to fret. That much, anyway.

Yet.

After Hugh and I wandered back inside—well, I wandered back inside while Hugh stayed out on the deck and lit a joint—Harrison asked me if he could drive me home.

"I have my mom's car," I admitted. God, it was bright in that kitchen. Stars were forming at the corners of my vision.

"Yeah, but you're not driving like that. Come on. I'll drop you and your car off, and then I'll walk home. I'm only a few blocks over from you."

"How do you know where I live?" I asked, a glimmer of hope resurfacing.

"Because of Christian. Everyone knew Christian Cummings," he added, like that should have been obvious.

Of course.

I was quiet most of the drive home, thinking. Annoyed that I had to even think of my brother right at that moment. I felt sort of hollow about what had happened between me and Hugh. I knew that if either of us had been sober, it wouldn't have happened. Or at least he wouldn't have gone up my—no, no, scratch that. He wouldn't have even kissed me in the first place. And I was struck, really struck, by the reminder that I wasn't the kind of girl that sober guys wanted to kiss. And what did "half-cute" even mean?

Harrison would never want to kiss me, drunk or sober.

All the same, I felt a new kind of tension between us. The last few weeks, I'd thought I felt a hint of electricity between us, maybe both of us too shy to make an actual move beyond our daily rounds of trading barbs. Now, though, I felt like I'd embarrassed him.

"What's wrong?" I finally muttered. After all, if I was *just a friend* to him, he should be straight with me.

"Nothing," he said flatly. Then after a moment of silence, he added, "I just didn't think Hugh would be your type."

Aaaand, now Harrison thinks I'm a slut, I realized. awesome.

Harrison turned onto my street and pulled into my driveway. He shifted the Buick into park, and looked at me, deciding how much to say.

"Hugh's my friend, but. You know," he eventually said, looking me in the eye. "I don't want you to get hurt."

I felt myself soften, like I'd been microwaved. Ding.

Maybe he was just looking out for me. That would be really sweet of him.

But then I hardened right back up—like I'd been left too long *in* the microwave.

Too late for that, I remembered. *"She's just a friend."*

"Whatever," I mumbled, as we both climbed out of the car and locked the doors. "I'll see you next week."

I soon learned that Hugh's parents were quite the travelers, and he held a party for the lacrosse team just about every Saturday. The following Tuesday, he'd gotten my number from Harrison and texted me an invite. When I read the text, my stomach twinged with the same feeling I recognized from that Saturday night. I knew I shouldn't want to go; in fact, I should probably steer clear of Hugh altogether and delete the text right away. But what other offers were on tap for me? And a guy who thought I was half-cute and wanted to make out with me—well, that was better than nothing. Right?

So next, I casually asked Harrison in Spanish if he was planning to go.

"Probably," he said nonchalantly. "You want a ride?"

"Uh, sure," I said, raising an eyebrow. "You're cool with that?"

"Well. Hugh already asked if I'd bring you back," he said, a barely perceptible edge to his voice.

And then again, the twinge in my stomach was back.

The next two Saturdays played out similarly to the previous one, though the drinking games changed up each time, and my tolerance grew slightly stronger. Each time, I ended the night making out with Hugh on his back deck, not entirely sure how I got there. What I did learn, though, was that it was entirely possible to make out with a guy you weren't really into.

You just had to picture another guy in your head (Harrison) to get yourself through it. And little by little, I didn't necessarily like him more, but I liked having a place to be on Saturdays and having someone look forward to me. Or a piece of me, as it were. Even if I came home at night feeling…I don't even know. Guilty maybe, but of what exactly? I wasn't sure.

I was also starting to wonder what this "meant" Hugh and I were. I didn't have any classes with him and never even crossed paths with him during the school day, and we hardly texted each other at all. Most days, Ash would help me work up the nerve to text him a "Hey," and we'd analyze not only his response but also the length of the response and the delay in response time and dissect what it all could mean. I don't think even the physicists at Fermilab could have worked out the equations we came up with over this.

The winter dance was also coming up, but Hugh hadn't mentioned anything.

Two weeks before the dance, my mom asked me if I was planning to go.

"I'm not sure if I want to," I'd said, trying to seem like I didn't care.

"Ash has a boyfriend, right?" she cautiously pressed. "Maybe he could set you up with a friend."

"Uh, I don't think so."

"What about Harrison? You'd make a cute couple," she said with a wink.

"No," I said vehemently. "Not gonna happen."

"Why not? You hang out with him every weekend. Just go as friends."

"Not likely."

"And not that it matters, but his mom is Bunco friends with Mrs. Wahlstrom, and she says that Mrs. Dorsey is just a doll."

"*Mom*," I groaned.

"Okay, okay," she said, holding up her hands. "I'm just saying. He seems like such a great guy."

Don't remind me, I thought. And the problem was, Harrison *was* a great guy. He still gave me his full attention any time we were together. He and I were always perfectly at ease. We had too many inside jokes to count and could finish each other's sentences. But what it came down to was, I wasn't enough for him.

And as the cookie crumbled, I wasn't enough for Hugh either.

Feeling pretty lousy about that exchange with my mom that morning, and about how much it physically hurt to look at Harrison sometimes—especially when I'd had a beer or two in me—when Hugh and I went out to the deck that night, I mustered up all my courage and threw a Hail Mary.

"Are you going to the Winter Dance?" I whispered when he was kissing my neck.

"Hmm?" he mumbled into my skin.

I took a deep breath. "Are you going to the Winter Dance?" I repeated, a little more loudly.

He paused, let out a sigh, and said, "Yeah."

"Oh," I said, trying to keep the hurt out of my voice and failing.

Hugh kept lightly kissing my neck for another moment. I then worked up the nerve to add, "With who?"

He did have the decency to stop macking on me at this point.

"You probably don't know her," he said, looking at his arms. "She goes to Benet."

"I see," I said, stiffening.

"I've known her family forever," he added. "Her lakehouse is next to ours."

Well. Just call me the heel of bread in the loaf bag: not quite thrown in the trash but passed over for the better piece, again and again.

I suddenly felt really cold and folded my legs up toward my chin, hugging my knees. So aware that I was never anything more to him than my body. I wanted to throw up, and this time, it wasn't the alcohol.

An excruciatingly awkward moment of silence passed, until I said, "Um, I think I'm gonna see if Harrison is ready to go home."

"Cool," Hugh said, reaching into his pocket for his phone.

I slipped through the door and out of his life.

CHAPTER 6

The next weekend, Matt was holding a housewarming party at his new apartment. His parents had kicked him out of the house and, being 19 and working nights driving for Lyft (my heart goes out to anyone in his backseat…anyway), he'd just co-signed on a one-step-up-from-a-landfill kind of place. Ash begged me to come with her since we'd barely hung out at all for the past month or so that she'd been with Matt. So, in the interest of being a good friend, and since I sure as hell wasn't ever going back to Hugh's house, I did.

Have you ever gone to a party and the minute you walked in your first instinct was to turn right around? Well, I probably should have.

The crowd consisted of a few of Matt's friends who looked, and there's no polite way to say it, *old*—I'm talking like, mid-twenties, maybe even thirties—some of their heavily tattooed girlfriends chain-smoking on the balcony and doing shots of cheap vodka, and a couple guys in the corner, stoned out of their minds and playing video games.

And, Matt's roommate, Scott, rounding out the bunch.

He was really tall, with a linebacker build, and a slight paunch that came with the death of exercising. He had sandy blonde hair, stubble and smelled of off-brand cologne and Southern Comfort.

He also spent most of the night finding excuses to talk to me, and when we were both on the couch, he had his arm along the back of it, just inches from my skin, sliding closer and closer to my shoulders each time he'd return it after taking a drink.

He did manage to keep his eyes on mine rather than on my chest, so that made him seem like a prince compared to Hugh. But, while he seemed like a decent enough person, he was at least five years too old for me, so *definitely* not someone I could ever take home to meet my parents.

At the end of the night, Scott asked me, uber-politely, if he could take me out to dinner sometime. I hesitated. He *was* being extremely nice toward me. He *was* asking me on a real date, something that had happened to me approximately never. He *was* gainfully employed (at a Verizon store, I think). But he was, by default, kind of an old creeper, too.

I gave him a wan smile and said, "You know what? I'll be back in a sec."

I got off the couch and went to look for Ash. I found her in the kitchen, spraying down the counters with cleaner and scrubbing out the beer can rings.

I raised an eyebrow at her.

"He'll never do it himself, and he'll lose his deposit otherwise," she said defensively.

Just then, I heard Matt call out from across the apartment, "Ash! Beer me!"

"One sec, babe!" she called back, still facing me. "What's up?"

"Scott's asking me if I want to go to dinner sometime."

"Ooh! You should!" she said, clasping her hands together.

"You think?" I said, voice full of doubt. "I don't know that he's…" my voice trailed off and I waved my hand around in a circle.

Ash folded her arms across her chest.

"You don't know that he's what?"

"My type," I finally said.

"Well, he's a hell of a lot nicer to you than your most recent guy. Cough, cough, Hugh."

I sighed. "Don't remind me." Right now, Hugh was probably picking out a $25 corsage for that Benet girl—the one that apparently *was* good enough to take out in public.

She gave my shoulder a squeeze. "Hey. You deserve a good guy, too," she said.

Matt's voice called out again, a little more impatient. "Ash! The hell are you waiting for, Christmas?"

Her lips tightened into a line, and she wordlessly pulled out two cans of Bud Light from the case on the floor, then headed back into the party.

I'd almost—*almost*—talked myself into going back into that room.

And I looked at Scott, sitting on the couch next to Matt. He was eyeballing a girl across the room—a girl with kohl eyeliner, purple lipstick, and braces, sipping a beer. She looked *maybe* 14, but I'd venture a guess that she was hoping to pass for 22. They made eye contact, and I kid you not, *he licked his lips.*

That snapped me right back into reality.

He, along with every guy in the room, sucked at life. I didn't deserve a prick like Hugh, but I didn't deserve a pedophile like Scott, either.

I deserve a great guy, dammit, a little voice inside me said. One great guy in particular.

I left without even saying goodbye to Ash. I knew I had to do it now or I'd lose my nerve.

I hopped in the car and drove right over to Harrison's house. His bedroom light was on. Either he hadn't gone to Hugh's that night, or he'd come back early. Didn't know. Didn't care.

I texted him.

Hey, I'm the neighborhood. Come outside.

A few seconds later, he fiddled with his blinds, then peered through the window. He had a look of recognition once he saw it was my mom's car—and me inside it. He threw a sweatshirt on over his tee and headed out the door. Less than a minute later, he was trotting down his driveway toward me.

I rolled down my window.

"Hop in," I said.

He dutifully did.

"So, did you go to Hugh's tonight?" I asked.

He wrinkled his nose. "Nah," he said, shrugging.

"No?"

"Kinda over that scene, I guess," he admitted. "What have you been up to?"

"I went to a party at Ash's boyfriend's place and it…well, it sucked," I said, half-laughing. "Completely sucked, really."

"Oh?"

"Oh, yeah." I filled him on the details of Matt. And also found myself pouring out my sadness about seeing the change in Ash.

"I just don't know what she sees in him," I lamented. "It's like he has this weird power over her, and the worse he treats her, the more she likes him."

He chuckled. "Some of us are just gluttons for punishment, I guess," he said, looking down at his feet. I wondered if he was thinking about Mara. Probably.

We were quiet for a minute. Companionably so, though.

It was now or never.

"Anyway, *amigo*," I said, trying my best to sound casual, despite my pinkening face.

"Yeah?"

"So. Um. Winter dance is coming up and all."

He looked politely at me.

"Do you want to, um, go? Like, as friends? As you know, *vecinos en clase?"* I added, rushing out the words and looking him in the neck.

I didn't hear an answer for a few seconds, and slowly brought my eyes to meet his face. He was smiling.

"Sure," he said, with the grin I knew and loved.

CHAPTER 7

Ash is a good enough friend that she'd usually listen to me talk about Harrison like a song on repeat. But, when I told her everything the next morning, she politely applauded my initiative before smacking just a little sense into me.

"Keep your guard up, you know? In case he ends up being an asshat."

"He wouldn't," I said defensively. "He's always been totally friendly toward me. Or flirty, even."

"That's because he's slot-machining you," Ash said matter-of-factly.

"He's what?"

"He's being a slot machine," she explained. "Those things suck people in because they pay out *only* just enough to keep someone hooked. The rest of the time, people just put in their money, over and over, getting nothing in return. As soon as the victim's about to walk away, they put in one last quarter, and what do you know? The machine doles out a tiny jackpot. Which makes them sit there and throw their money away for hours on end."

I was silent.

"He's stringing you along because he can," Ash clarified. "He enjoys it that you like him."

"You're just mad I didn't want to go out with Scott," I retorted.

"Well, Scott was at least direct about liking you," she said airily. "Harrison hasn't been."

"First of all, Scott was looking at that little freshman like he wanted to impregnate her mouth. I'm not going anywhere near him. And second, maybe going to the dance will change things with me and Harrison."

Ash looked at me sympathetically. "If you say so," she finally said.

Hmph. Not like *she* had any right to say any of that—talk about the pot calling the kettle black. Matt was getting worse and worse to her all the time. He treated her like a maid or worse. Last night was bad enough. The week before, she complained to me that he made her run to the grocery store to restock his Doritos supply so he and his gamer friends wouldn't have to interrupt their Fallout marathon. When I'd asked her why she didn't just say no, she'd shrugged and said, "Well, I was the only one not playing."

That moron Matt never realized that out of the two of them, *she* was the catch. The sad thing is, Ash didn't realize it either. And not for the first time, I'd wondered if had the whole Homecoming weekend never happened, if Seamus Dean never happened, how different things would be for her.

But, being Ash's best friend, I didn't say any of that to her. She'd figure it out on her own eventually. I hoped.

At any rate, I couldn't dwell on her lust life. I had the dance with Harrison coming up.

Within a few more texts with him, everything was soon set. We weren't going out to dinner beforehand, because Harrison had a box lacrosse tournament that day and wouldn't get back until 8. He offered to just meet me at the dance since he'd be dropped back off at the school anyway, and I agreed (a little sad about no pre-dance pictures, but not much I could do about it. Anyway, we were going as friends. Ok, as friend and one-sided crush masquerading as friend.). I wasn't gonna third-wheel it at dinner with Matt and Ash, but she and I planned to meet up as soon as we each got to the dance.

It felt a little anticlimactic to know I'd arrive by myself, but the butterflies and anticipation kept me going. Because I had decided that I was finally going to let Harrison know how I felt about him.

I'd run it over in my head hundreds of times how it could potentially go: maybe we'd be slow dancing to a song, and lock eyes, and both lean in for a kiss. Maybe it would be when I dropped him off at the end of the night, and the hug would linger too long. Maybe I'd just blurt out, "Harrison, I want to be with you." But, I knew I had to do *something* at this point. As much as I loved the friendship we had, I couldn't keep living my life as it was, hopelessly wondering if we could ever turn into more.

That night, I was dressed to the damn nines. I had on a short, black sequined cocktail dress and four-inch stilettos that I borrowed from my mom. They took practice to walk in, but Harrison was well over six feet, and in order to make this kiss in my head come true...well, a couple of laps around the kitchen would be worth it. My hair was cooperating, and the flatiron had done its magic; and, I'd watched endless YouTube videos on how to perfect my eye make-up. I looked good—definitely the most grown-up I'd ever looked before. The Jennifer Aniston all-in-black awards show look—glam, but classic.

Mom was legit thrilled that I was going with Harrison, so she yanked me into the car to go dress shopping the minute I told her that he was my date. She was also letting me borrow the Enclave for the evening. I was already having inappropriate ideas about what could go on in that Enclave when I drove Harrison home.

I was about to pull on my coat and grab the keys when Mom stopped me.

"Just wait a sec," she said, pulling out her phone. "I gotta take some pictures for Dad."

"Oh, God," I muttered, but obediently posed for a few pictures by the front door anyway. Dad was at a conference in Phoenix this weekend. Which might have been for the best, since I'm not entirely sure he would have let me out the door in those heels.

"What can I say, I have the most beautiful daughter in Snow Ridge," she clucked proudly, tapping away before posting it.

"Hardly," I said, rolling my eyes, but finding myself blushing.

"You'll always be beautiful to me, my little star of Bethlehem," she said, kissing the top of my head. "Inside and out."

She hadn't called me that in years. Actually, she hadn't shown this much interest in me or my life in years. Was it because the fact that I was going to a dance, with a date, was something she could finally get excited about?

She tugged my dress down a half inch and then smiled. "And Harrison better recognize that."

"Okay, I'm leaving now," I said. I was touched that she said that—but, you know, not enough to say anymore. And I had somewhere I needed to be.

CHAPTER 8

Just before 8 PM, I pulled into the school's parking lot, took a deep breath, and walked amidst the crowds into Snow Ridge High. I waited at the edge of the hallway near the fieldhouse, where Harrison and I had planned to meet.

A few minutes went by, and I furiously scrolled through Instagram and tried to look busy as waves of people paraded by me. Each of them in groups, each of them with their dates.

The seconds crawled by, and it was 8:10. I pulled my belted wool coat tighter into myself, wishing I could disappear. I texted Harrison, *I'm here. You on your way?* hoping I didn't come across as freaked out as I felt.

Nothing.

A few more moments passed, and the crowds passing me by began to thin. Every one of these thoughts went through my head on repeat:

- He's ghosting me.
- He broke his ankle at the tournament, and he's at some hospital in Barrington or wherever.
- The bus got into an accident, and they all died on impact.
- His phone died.
- He forgot.
- He hates me.
- He thinks I'm a complete loser.
- He only said yes because he felt bad for me.
- He's not coming.

It then occurred to me that Ash wasn't here, either, and I immediately friend-shamed myself. I was about to text her when I heard footsteps jogging down the hall.

Harrison.

I couldn't help it—I broke into a huge grin. He was in a charcoal gray suit that looked like it was made for him, a white shirt, a black tie, and his hair was glistening.

"Hey, Bethany," he said, giving me a quick peck on the cheek in greeting (!). "Sorry, the bus got back here kinda late and I had to shower."

(Swoon. I tried to keep from thinking of him in the shower. And failed.)

"No worries," I said coolly. "I just got here anyway. Wanna go in?"

"Let's do it," he said, and put his hand gently on my lower back (!) as we walked down the hall to the ticket table.

We entered the fieldhouse and were greeted by blaring music and over a thousand people already going crazy on the dance floor.

"Can I take your coat?" Harrison asked, ever the gentleman.

I shrugged myself out of it, and I saw his eyes widen slightly in appreciation at my dress.

"Damn, girl," he said, letting out a low whistle. "You clean up nice."

"This? It's old," I said with a laugh.

Dammit, I couldn't even take a compliment right.

I was about to hand my coat to him when I felt the phone buzz in my pocket.

"Oh, wait," I said, and grabbed my phone. It was Ash. And she was calling instead of texting?

"One sec," I apologized, and scooted toward the hall where the music wasn't deafening.

"Ash, what's up?" I said upon answering.

Even with the noise, I could hear her crying. "Bethany?"

"What happened?" I asked, my heart beating faster.

"He left me," she sobbed. "He's such a dumbass, and he lit up a joint in the car, and we got into a huge fight about it, and *he left me*. On the side of Ogden Avenue. In the freaking snow!"

"What?!" I yelled. "That jerk!"

"Can you get me?" she cried. "Like, now?"

"Yes. Oh, my God. Of course. What intersection are you at?"

She gave me the details, and I promised I'd leave immediately.

I ran back into the fieldhouse to tell Harrison, who was already chatting with some of the guys from lacrosse. As I sputtered out the story, he was just as horrified as I was.

"Do you want me to come with you?" he asked, concerned.

"No, no," I insisted. "She probably doesn't want anyone to see her like this. I'll be back as soon as I can. Probably with Ash."

"Okay," he said cautiously. "If you're sure."

"I'm sure," I confirmed.

I threw my coat back on, darted to my car, and raced toward Ash, cursing Matt's name as I drove.

About five minutes later, I found Ash at the stoplight, and she ran to my car. She was shivering in her vintage blue silk dress—she'd gone jacketless, and her hair and makeup already looked bedraggled from the combination of tears and sleet.

"Oh, honey," I said, wrapping her in my coat as she wordlessly cried. We pulled into an empty parking lot, and she poured her heart out while I kept handing her tissues and holding her hand.

"Why does this always happen to me?" she bawled.

"I don't know," I said sympathetically. "Because guys are jerks?"

She looked down at her nails. "Not guys like Harrison." Then her eyes widened in realization. "Oh, crap. Harrison is at the dance, waiting for you, isn't he?"

"It's okay," I insisted. "This is more important."

"*No*," she said, wiping her eyes. "No way. You've been waiting for this chance for months. I'm not screwing it up for you."

"You're not screwing anything up for me." Matt, on the other hand…

"We're going to the dance," Ash said, snapping the visor down and popping open the mirror. She rummaged in her purse and began to reapply her lip gloss. "Start driving."

"We don't have to—"

"*Drive!*"

So I did. We got back to the dance within the next ten minutes, gave ourselves a once-over for approval, and headed in.

It was even busier inside now, and the music continued to shake the fieldhouse.

"Do you see Harrison anywhere?" I yelled over the din.

"Not yet, but I'm looking," Ash yelled back.

Our eyes scanned the room as we walked arm in arm, looking for him.

Then I finally saw him, off toward the corner. God, he looked so amazing in that suit. As I walked toward him, all my scenarios came back rushing to me. I felt a little nauseous. I felt warm and fuzzy all over. I felt like it was going to happen for me, for us—I just *knew* it.

And as I got closer, I saw who he was talking to slightly leaning over her, with his hand reaching to pull a strand of golden hair off her face.

Mara. His ex. Who was *supposed* to be three hours away in Madison but had evidently decided to show up here for some reason.

Well. Not *some* reason.

She was in a tight, red dress, showing off every one of her assets. Her makeup was artfully done. She looked like she'd just stepped off a damn runway.

Then, she looked at Harrison like a Disney princess looks at her prince—and leaned up to kiss him.

And he definitely kissed back.

Ash saw it, too. Her arm clenched mine tighter.

"What the actual?" she growled. "I'm gonna kill him."

"Don't," I whispered, and turned on my heels, speed-walking toward the girls' room. Ash trailed me into the handicapped stall and hugged me while I started to cry.

"It's gonna be okay," she murmured. "And he's just an idiot who doesn't deserve you, anyway."

"That's not true," I said, sniffling. "He's just in love with someone else. And he's never going to feel for me what I feel for him."

Ash sighed and hugged me a little closer.

"You don't know that," she said. "But my God, the sheer *nerve* of her. They effing broke up!"

Just then, we heard more footsteps clack into the bathroom and the sound of tinkling voices, chattering away. I glanced at

Ash and put my finger to my lips—I didn't need any attention right now.

After a few seconds, a girl's voice came through clearly amid the din.

"Did you see that Mara Frost is here?" she asked. My heart started to pound, and Ash and I looked at each other expectantly.

"Yeah, she came back for Harrison, to make some grand gesture or whatever," a voice answered back. Without even seeing her, I could tell it was Lindsay talking. She added, "It's funny. He was really basic back at Middle, but he's improved. *Clearly*."

"Yeah, I wouldn't kick him out of bed," the other girl said, laughing.

"I don't think Mara will, either." More snickering.

Ash's hands tightened into fists, and she raised her eyebrows, silently saying, *Let me at them.* I shook my head and mouthed, *No.*

"Who'd he come with, anyway?" Lindsay asked. "His date's gotta be pissed."

"Um, Bethany Cummings, I think?" the other girl replied.

Lindsay snorted. "Oh. Well, who cares then?"

"Right?" the other girl agreed with a laugh.

They clacked out of the bathroom, and as soon as they were out of earshot, I puked. Ash rubbed my back until I straightened myself up, wiped my eyes with the back of my hand, and said, "Let's go."

CHAPTER 9

Bringing us back to the McDonald's parking lot, about half an hour later.

"All right, explain,'" I said, cocking an eyebrow. "Tell me how we're gonna magically solve the problem of getting ditched and humiliated at the winter dance."

"No, MENSA-pants," Ash said. "We're taking this a lot further than some stupid dance. What happened at the dance is not the disease. It's a *symptom* of the disease."

"Huh?"

Her gleaming eyes were darting back and forth. Clearly, her wheels were turning.

"See, here's the thing," she said. "You're right. We can do everything 'perfectly'—the way we dress, the way we act, what we say, everything. We can—and do—bend over freaking backwards for these guys. And in the end, it doesn't even matter, because they have all the power. True?"

I didn't say anything but nodded glumly. She was voicing everything I'd been thinking for 16 years, but I was too devastated by Harrison to form actual words at the moment.

"And why, exactly, do they walk all over us like this? Spreading rumors about us? Passing us over for 'better' girls? And not only the guys, but teachers! Relatives! The whole freaking Snow Ridge patriarchy! *Why do they think they're superior to us*?"

"If you're gonna give a speech about low self-esteem, now's really not the time—"

"Because we believe them!" Ash practically roared, cutting me off. "And that stops *right this minute.*"

"Wait, what?" Now I was really puzzled.

"We—and not just you and me, but most girls in this town—take second-class citizenship to an advanced art form," Ash said, shaking her head. "Basically, we've done nothing but think, 'What can I do to make him like me?' When, for the love of God, why aren't we thinking instead, 'Hmm, what can *he* do to make me like *him*?'"

It was like a damn light bulb finally went off inside my head.

"I have no good answer for that," I said, incredulous. "Honestly, I've seen a lot of egregious crap in this town, but I've never thought to ask myself specifically *that*."

"Right?!" Ash said. "It's crazy. And this stupid town has, like, shot our confidence to hell in a handbasket. Especially after what happened with Dane and Seamus. It felt like I wasn't good enough for anybody, and I found myself with a total loser. And the next thing I knew, I was at Matt's beck and call, praying, 'I sure hope I can hold onto him.' And for what?"

"The amazing 'prize' of his temporary company?" I muttered.

"Or getting treated like crap for a couple months and then literally left by the side of the road?" Ash cried, her voice rising to a crescendo. "Seriously, what's worse?"

"How about getting mixed messages for months, only to find him kissing the girl he *really* likes right in front of your face?" I spat.

"Never again!" Ash shouted.

"Never!" I agreed, and we furiously hugged.

After a moment, I said into Ash's hair, "Um. Ash?"

"Yeah?" she asked, pulling back.

"So, how's this gonna work exactly, that we don't put up with this garbage anymore…?"

"Oh! Yeah," she said brightly. "The two problems we're anointed to solve: the way we're treated, and the fact that we take it. Well, here's how I see it. This problem is systemic. So we can keep playing by their crappy traditional rules and nothing changes. Or, we can reinvent the game."

I was beyond skeptical. "You think we can just somehow turn, like, more than 100 years of tradition on its head."

"Why not?" she countered. "Happens in politics all the time. Hello, look at the last election. Anything—and anyone—can be manipulated by someone with power. Or by someone who *believes* in their own power."

"There's that," I agreed.

"B," she continued. "Just think. How many girls do you think go to Snow Ridge?"

"Total? Maybe around 1,000?"

"*Precisely*," she confirmed. "How many of them are treated like equals by their boyfriends? None. But they can't *all* buy into the Snow Ridge Stepford wife in training nonsense. I'm not talking bought-in bitches like Lindsay, but there must be *hundreds* of girls who, deep-down, feel like we do and would like to take these guys down a notch or five. People aren't as happy as they make it look online."

"Fine. Maybe we're not alone, but I don't --"

"Just think of how fab it would feel to give guys in this town a taste of their own medicine," she said. "And to systematically dismantle their crappy hierarchy, piece by piece." For effect, she sprinkled the confetti-sized remains of her McDonald's napkin out the window and smirked.

I wrinkled my nose. "I still don't know about this, Ash. Just because we see a problem doesn't mean we're qualified to solve it. I mean, come on. I also see that climate change is a problem, but that doesn't mean I can figure out the solution to that one, either, you know?"

She shrugged. "Suit yourself," she said. "But I'm gonna get to work on figuring this out, stat. I don't want to be at the mercy of their whims anymore. And I don't think you do, either."

I closed my eyes and the last few years of sad and sorry treatment came rushing back—not just from Harrison, but from every male in this godforsaken town. The teachers, so many of whom would call on a boy with his hand raised before calling on a girl. Guys like Shane and Hugh, who never looked at me as more than low-hanging fruit. Total jerks like Seamus, who thought they had the right to grope any girl they wanted, and guys like Dane, who were fine with letting that kind of thing slide. But in the end, what hurt most was Harrison, who *had* to know how much I cared about him and stabbed me right in the heart anyway, Making him probably the worst of all.

I took a deep breath. "Okay," I said. "Let's figure this out. Because you're my bestie, and I got you. Ride or die."

"Ride or die," Ash agreed, wiping away a tear.

CHAPTER 10

The next day started winter break, so Ash and I got together to brainstorm. After holing ourselves up in her bedroom, I started tapping away at a new document on my phone, and we got to work.

"Okay," I said. "How're we supposed to start?"

Ash pursed her lips and tapped her chin.

"It's gonna have to be a multi-pronged approach, for sure," she affirmed. "Seeing as how many things are totally unjust here. And how many girls we need to flip over from the dark side."

"Okay. How are we supposed to do that?" I prodded.

"Become internet famous?" she said wryly. "Start a vlog bitching about Snow Ridge guys?"

I chuckled. "I was thinking we could start a feminists club at school or something."

"There's that," she acknowledged. "Though, I don't know. Problem is, 'feminist' is a dirty word in this town, and it's gonna scare people away. And even if we gave it some other euphemism, is that the kind of thing that's going to make us really, and I hate to use this word, popular? Like, would it really raise us from bottom bitch status?"

"We're not bottom bitches," I countered.

Ash gave me a hard look. "B, I hate to break it to you, but that's *exactly* what we are."

I let out a sigh. "This hopeless."

"It doesn't have to be," Ash insisted. "We're gonna figure it out. I promise. And when the answer hits us, we're gonna know."

We hadn't figured it out by Christmas, but we were taking a break from talking about it that day—mostly, because we were engaging in forced family interaction all day. Mom was beyond depressed that Christian was still going to be in Australia over the holidays ("It's my first Christmas *without* my baby!" she wailed more than once, conveniently forgetting that *I* was her youngest child, but whatever). To appease her, Dad suggested we all wake up early and open our presents at 7 AM and video call Christian, so that at least we could celebrate Christmas "together" on the actual day.

So, at just after 7, I found myself dragged out of bed and heading downstairs, where Christian awaited us from the TV screen, swinging in his hammock with the ocean behind him, and sipping from an amber bottle. Dad had gotten Mom an Apple TV and set it up for her last night, just for this purpose.

"Hey, Christian," I said. "Working hard or hardly working?"

"Shut up, Breathany. It's Christmas and I've earned it."

"Oh, I bet. Must be real hard slapping some paint on the occasional wall when you're so hungover."

I'd seen his posts. There were like two from Habitat for every dozen on the beach or at the bar.

"For your information, I'm doing a lot more than 'slapping paint on a wall,'" he retorted. "Have you ever hung drywall? Installed laminate flooring? Laid tile? All so that homeless families could have a roof over their head? No? Didn't think so."

I rolled my eyes and started preparing my clapback, but Mom came in with a tray of cinnamon rolls and insisted we start opening presents.

To his credit, Christian sent us a box of presents that had arrived a couple of weeks ago. I'd ordered him a new Swiss Army knife off of Amazon last week, threw in the extra bucks for wrapping and expedited shipping, and crossed my fingers it would get there in time. Maybe I loathed him most of the time, but it was Christmas, and we would usually try to get each other semi-decent gifts and act like we cared about each other for a few hours.

Christmas wasn't a huge, massive holiday for our family—I mean, we were well off by a lot of standards, but our parents didn't go overboard. In fact, Mom and Dad had a $100 limit to spend on each of us to keep things fair. I lucked out by getting a $100 gift card to my favorite local bookstore, and I already had a list in mind of books I'd get with it. Christian had just asked Mom and Dad for the money, which he got, and he seemed to genuinely like the Swiss Army knife from me.

"Already coming in handy," he said, using the bottle opener on his next beer. Mom tutted but smiled anyway.

"Looks like you've got the last one," Dad said, pointing to my box from Christian.

"Oh, right," I said, pulling it onto my lap. I started tearing off the paper, revealing a cardboard box. I sliced open the tape with my fingernails and opened it to see…a Macbook?

"You got me a *Macbook?*"

He smiled. "Well, when Mom and Dad got me a new one, I didn't think I needed two."

I whipped my head toward my parents. "You got him a new Macbook? When?"

"September maybe?" Mom said, trying to remember. "He needed a new one. The old one kept freezing, and he needed a better camera for video calls."

"So this is Christian's old—and basically broken—computer. From like when you were in eighth grade," I said, clarifying and holding it up. "And you got him a new $1,500 computer, three months ago, so that he could see you better from the beach?"

Mom frowned at me.

No one else thought this was weird?

I looked at Christian. "You handed me down your five-year-old computer. For Christmas."

"You don't want it, you can send it back," he offered, narrowing his eyes.

"Bethany, he's volunteering for six months," Mom said sharply. "*For the homeless.* He can't afford to buy presents."

"Don't look a gift horse in the mouth," Dad added, without looking up from the Sports section he'd suddenly found.

"No, no," I said, holding up a hand. "Wow. Christian. Thank you for your undying generosity."

"Whatever," he muttered.

After we signed off with Christian, we went back up to our bedrooms, ostensibly to get some more sleep. However, I was going to get the computer set up to my liking. Yes, I had behaved like a brat, and I should have been glad I wouldn't have to use the household computer anymore but *come on.* In

Christian's mind, shipping it off to me was probably just easier than finding an electronics recycler in Brisbane.

I turned it on and plugged the battery pack in, and it whirred to life. The wallpaper was the Chicago Fire logo, which showed me that he hadn't even cleaned the computer back to factory settings. I shook my head at him.

Wow, thanks again for such a thoughtful gift. Dick.

I was about to Google precisely *how* to set it all back to default when I noticed the lower, far right icon on the screen. The trash can. And it wasn't empty.

Was he that lazy? Or just that incredibly stupid?

I clicked it open, because seriously, who wouldn't?

Not only wasn't it empty, it was full. In fact, it was 1,688 items full.

Well, I was nosy, but I wasn't about to snoop through 1,688 of my brother's photos and files. Even I'm not that desperate for entertainment.

But, I was gonna go through at least *some* of them.

After being sufficiently grossed out by the first two photos I opened, I dragged them all into a Photos subfolder without opening the rest and planned to throw them out in one fell swoop. The word docs, meh, the first few I opened were pretty boring and clearly just papers he'd written in high school. I would have considered keeping one or two for reference, except I'd probably already written my own paper on whatever subject it was and had gotten a better grade than he did. Same thing with the handful of PowerPoints.

But the spreadsheets. Well, that's where it got interesting.

Let me reiterate that Christian was *not* an amazing student by any stretch of the imagination. He got through all of his classes, with my parents and his tutors making sure his grades were high enough to keep him on the soccer team. He didn't see the point in honors classes—not that he'd have gotten into any—since he assumed he'd get a college scholarship thanks to his athletic ability (and he'd been right). And in the end, all of us knew he'd just end up working for Dad one day. So as long as he could read, write, add and subtract, what else did he really need?

This spreadsheet I found—labeled simply, "POINT SYSTEM"—required just those four educational skills. But it also required a cold, twisted mind. The first page of it outlined a very detailed scoring matrix. I read it and re-read it, peering closely. Christian evidently had come up with a scoring system to rate girls at Snow Ridge. Not rating them on their looks, or bodies, or anything like that. No, no. This was *much* more devious.

He scored them based on their actions toward him. A hug or a text, according to Christian, was each worth 2 points. A kiss, 5 points. A handy meant 10 points—the same point value he assigned to "attending an away soccer game."

I couldn't look, and I couldn't *not* look.

Then, I moved on to the second page of the spreadsheet and, sure enough, he had individual columns for twenty-four, no wait, *twenty-five* girls. They weren't listed alphabetically, but just from memory, I quickly realized that they were listed chronologically. They were lined up in order from when Christian dated them, or took them to a dance, or—well, about half of them I had never seen with him in public, so I guess he'd hooked up with them in secret. I tried not to look much at the far-left column, where it listed things like "blow jobs" and "up the shirt." The last thing I wanted was to paint a vivid picture of each girl.

But the really interesting thing? Each girl had a total of *exactly* 100.

I was perplexed for a moment. Like, if a girl got 100 points, wouldn't that mean she got 100%, making her an A+? And if that was the case, why would there be more than one girl even on the sheet?

And then it dawned on me. For all the girls he dated, Christian had never, ever been upset about a breakup with any one of them. He never seemed to care deeply about any of them. He only dated a girl for a few weeks tops. He'd never had his heart broken.

It was so clear now: he had *always* been the heartbreaker. As soon as a girl got to 100 points, *he dumped her.*

I felt nauseated for a moment. Ashamed to be even related to him. Then furious that he did this to twenty-five human beings. Not like these girls were ever my friends or anything, but sheesh, no one deserved that. To score girls, and then dump them for the crime of trying to form an actual relationship? To treat girls like total crap? Who the hell did he think he was?

A genius, said a little voice inside my head. *With power.*

Oh my God, I thought. *That's it.*

I didn't see Ash at all that day because, again, forced family togetherness time and whatnot. But the next morning, I jogged to her house, Macbook in my backpack, and rang her doorbell at 10 AM.

She opened the door and found me, eyes flashing and pink in the face.

"Ash," I said, slightly out of breath. "You know how you said that when we found the answer to our whole Snow Ridge guy problem, we'd know it?"

A smile crept on her face.

"Tell me."

CHAPTER 11

After I showed her the spreadsheet Christian had made, and explained the conclusions I'd reached, she was just as revolted as I was.

"Sick, right?" I agreed. "Anyone who would do that clearly had no effs to give about the people he scored."

"Exactly," she agreed. "But what does this have to do with us?"

"Ash. Aren't you the one who said that *we* should be out of effs to give? And this is a—a—*blueprint* on how to act that way. We won't stand for a moment of crap treatment anymore—that's a given. But to really get the power, we need to not even ultimately reward the *good* behavior. We have to get savage. Be the one in the relationship with the upper hand, you know?"

The lightbulb went on in her head, too.

"You know what? That's a fair point," she agreed. "Copy that spreadsheet and we'll use it as a template."

"And set our own rules," I affirmed.

"Right," she agreed, excited. "Ooh. Okay. How many points does it take before we dump their asses? Or I guess, if we're not dating them, to just kick them to the curb and start ignoring them?"

"Why re-invent the wheel? How about an even 100?"

"Beautiful. Type that in," she instructed, gesturing toward my laptop.

I typed that in.

"Now, let's come up with achievements and their point values," I said.

"Great," said Ash. "How about...taking us on an actual date, that's 10 points."

"Really? I was thinking more like 20," I said. "Consider what we're working with."

"Well, okay," she agreed. "That's 20. How about a gift of any kind, that's 10 points."

"Perfect," I said, typing away. "I'm thinking a genuine compliment is five points. How's that?"

"I like it," she said. "Hmm. How about a phone call?"

"Ha," I said, my voice dripping with sarcasm. "That's like 50."

"Nope and nope," she said. "I'm bringing the phone call back."

"Why?" I asked, wrinkling my nose.

"Because if a guy really wants to work for me, then I don't want every interaction I have with him to consist of a bunch of typos and emojis," she said vehemently. "I want him to actually *talk* to me and care about what I think and have to say. Ten points. Tops."

"Okay," I said, not willing to argue further. "Ten it is."

"How about doing you a solid favor? Like, he gives you a ride home or quizzes you to prep for a test, something like that?"

"Five," I said, typing that in.

"Can you think of anything else we should add?"

"How about a blanket category for chivalrous acts?

"Doesn't that sound all patriarchy-y?"

"Not like that," I explained. "Like, doing the things you would do to show someone you're a polite human. Maybe opening the car door for someone, or letting you in the elevator first."

"God, that sets the bar low," Ash groaned.

I shrugged. "Well, look at who we're dealing with."

"True. Okay, those can be two each," Ash confirmed. "Think we should cap it off here to start?"

"This is probably good for now," I said. "But it's a working document. We can add to it at any time."

"Exactly," Ash said, her eyes flashing with delight. "And I'm sure we will be."

I smirked. "No doubt. But I think there's one thing we're overlooking."

"What's that?"

"Bad behavior."

"Ooh, good *point*," she said. "Ba-dum ching."

"Christian was too dumb to think of this, but I'm thinking we should have a system to automatically eliminate people when necessary."

"Absolutely," she said, nodding vigorously. "This kind of thing would have nipped me and Matt in the bud. Before he dumped me by ditching me on the side of the road in the rain. In December."

"Exactly. Though, I have a feeling we're not gonna know what the bad behavior is until we see it. Because you never know what kind of awful thing a guy's capable of until he actually does it."

"Ain't that God's honest truth," she muttered.

We both pondered that for a moment.

"So, let's just make a note that they can always get automatically disqualified for something that's just despicable," I said.

"Perfect."

"Of course," I added, "let's hope this system knocks them out of the running before the despicable-level behavior even happens, though."

"I sure hope so," she said.

I finished typing and then we reviewed the list.

"I kind of feel like we should get someone on the board right away. You know, to test it out. Like have a control group," Ash explained.

I scratched my head. "Well, I guess we could kinda review in our heads to use someone from before, like Dane or Hugh or something. We could go point by point, and then tally up, so we'd realize the optimal time to dump them before they hurt us."

"Nah," Ash said, shaking her head. "That's in the past, and I don't know about you, but having to remember that stuff just leaves a bad taste in my mouth."

"True," I admitted.

"I think we just have to go onward and upward," she said. "And I've got the perfect test subject."

"Who?"

"Trevor Chen."

I coughed.

"Seriously?"

Trevor Chen was like a guidance counselor's dream come true: volleyball player, golf team captain, member of Peer Jury, finalist at the statewide science fair, National Merit Scholar extraordinaire and known for his early acceptance to University of Chicago this coming fall. Not only that, he could lay on the charm like nobody's business. *And*, he had been Lindsay's date to the winter dance.

"Why Trevor Chen?" I asked, totally puzzled. "He's such a nice guy."

"Exactly. He's basically perfect and should score well, hypothetically, so we should have something to compare everyone else to. Plus, I think I have a shot at nailing this in the first go-round."

"How's that?"

"Oh, you know," she said with a wink. "My feminine wiles."

"Excuse me while I throw up in my mouth."

"No, for real! He was definitely flirty with me all last semester in gym class—though, I was too wrapped up in stupid Dane and then stupid Matt to even consider him. Plus, I am pretty sure Trevor has a thing for blondes."

That much was true—his girlfriend from last year, Diana Wilson (Wilson and Wilson, Attorneys at Law, Est. 1994) looked a heck of a lot like Ash—and Lindsay, for that matter. Diana had been on Homecoming Court, incidentally partnered up with Christian, and was now at U of I.

"The most important thing about Trevor, though," Ash continued, "Is that he will almost definitely be at Lindsay's New Year's party."

I raised an eyebrow. "What about Lindsay's New Year's party?" I asked cautiously.

"Well, you said she invites you every year—"

"Her *mom* tells *my mom* that I'm invited every year," I interrupted. "It's not like Lindsay invites me, and I never, ever go."

Ash smirked. "This time, you're going. That is, *we're* going."

I rolled my eyes. "Uh huh. So what am I allegedly going to do at this party while you're busy reeling in Trevor Chen?" I asked, dubious.

"He'll have friends with him," she insisted. "Take your pick."

"Right, because that's how it usually works out for me."

"Whichever one seems to like you the most, play it coolest with *that* one. Because that's the one who'll end up paying off most in the long run."

I eyed her warily.

"Trust me."

```
 The Point System:
2 points:
 Polite act (e.g opening a car door)
5 points:
 Genuine compliment
 Solid favor
 Sincere apology
10 points:
 Phone call
 Material gift
20 points:
 Actual date (he must invite, plan and
  pay)

Immediate dismissal:
 Egregious and unforgivable infractions
 (to be determined)

Addendum:
 No points to be awarded for polite and
 normal behavior as that is to be
 expected of any human being.
```

CHAPTER 12

First things first.

The next day, my doorbell rang. I peeked out the front window and saw that it was Mrs. Wahlstrom and Lindsay, each carrying a banker's box of wilting poinsettias. I took a deep breath, then threw on my biggest smile and answered the door.

"Hi!" I said, with all the enthusiasm I could muster and ushering them out of the flurries. "How was your Christmas?"

"Oh, it was the best, honey!" said Mrs. Wahlstrom, wrapping me in a one-armed hug before depositing the box on the floor. She was actually really sweet, always had been. It wasn't her fault that her daughter was born sour. "How was yours?"

"It was fine," I said. "Christian got me a pretty great gift." *A gift that'll keep on giving, I bet.*

Lindsay raised her eyes for just a second at the mention of Christian, but they were quickly lowered back down to her phone.

"Is your mom here?"

"You just missed her—she ran out to the grocery store."

"Oh, okay. Well, we just wanted to swing by with the extra poinsettias left over from the Juniors' sale." My mom was the treasurer of the Snow Ridge Junior Woman's Club. They were fairly liberal with the term "junior"—like, you had to be under 50. She had a few more years to go before she had to level up to the Snow Ridge Woman's Club.

"Thanks!" I said brightly. "I'm sure she has an idea of what she wants to do with them."

"Definitely," agreed Mrs. Wahlstrom. "So, you having a nice break? Any plans for New Year's?"

At this point, Lindsay shot her mom a "shut-up-let's-leave" look.

I cleared my throat.

"Actually, I was thinking I'd finally take you up on your party invite this year," I said, looking at Lindsay with a measured smile.

"You were?" she asked, a small blushflush creeping up her neck.

"That's great!" said Mrs. Wahlstrom, clasping her hands together.

"And I was thinking I'd bring my friend, Ash. As long as it's okay with you."

"Of course that's fine, sweetie," said Mrs. Wahlstrom.

Lindsay was trying so hard to remain calm that she looked physically pained.

"Sure," she said flatly.

"Well," said Mrs. Wahlstrom, still grinning. "We've gotta run but tell your mom I say hi and I'll see her at book club next week."

"Will do," I said as they headed toward their car. "See you real soon!"

And when New Year's Eve came just days later, Ash and I were ready as we'd ever be.

Getting to this night, I'll admit, was a smidgen painful. I'd already gone to the bookstore and bought four spankin' new hardcover novels to tide me over until Spring when Ash mentioned that it would be a good idea to show up at Lindsay's looking like a boss.

"You're right," I sighed. We *were* still females in Snow Ridge after all—we couldn't exactly launch our plan on just personality alone. So, with a heavy heart, I returned my books for the cash, and we headed for the mall.

We shopped, deliberated, tried on and ultimately got a badass outfit apiece. On our way to the exit, though, Ash suddenly stopped.

"You know, there's just one more thing I'm gonna do," she said, a gleam in her eye.

"What?"

She pulled me in the opposite direction until we were at the salon attached to the mall.

"Do you have anyone available for a haircut?" she asked the receptionist.

The receptionist scanned her computer.

"We actually just had a cancellation—Nia can do a cut and style right now."

"Perfect," said Ash.

Moments later, she was in the stylist's chair, and I was standing off to the side.

The stylist was finger-combing Ash's long, ice-blonde locks. "And what would you like—"

"Cut it all off," Ash interrupted.

Both of us looked at her quizzically, but Ash maintained her resolve.

"I want it short. Choppy. A little longer on one side. But all this length"—Ash gestured to the foot of cornsilk hair between her chin and her stomach—"I want it gone," Ash insisted.

I looked at Ash, then at the stylist with an air of authority.

"You heard the woman," I said.

We got back to my house and got to business getting ready. Ash was getting dressed in my room while I showered and changed in the bathroom. When I came back to my room and saw her, I was taken aback at the final look. Ash was wearing a backless, metallic gold dress with a brocade top and tulle lower half. She looked unbelievable, and she was staring in equal awe of me.

"Bethany. Oh, my gosh. You are *stunning."*

I'd taken my time with my makeup and flatironed my hair into sexy waves. I was in a champagne-colored ruffled blouse, a black pencil skirt and stiletto booties. The old me never would have pulled any of this off the rack. But seeing Ash look at me—and seeing myself in the mirror—I didn't look like a high school student, or even a college student, for that matter. I looked like a New Yorker on the job. And more than that, I felt like a badass bitch who wasn't going to take any crap from anyone—least of all, some lame-ass high school boy.

We had our new looks down—now we just had to make it past my parents on our way out. Our clothes weren't too revealing for them to object, but they definitely weren't standard Snow Ridge High fare.

Still, my parents looked at Ash and me a touch warily over their mugs of Bailey's as we came down the stairs.

"Wow, who kidnapped my daughter and replaced her with Sandra Bullock?" Dad asked.

"Dad, she's like 50," I said. "You're saying I look 50?"

"She's 50?" he asked Mom, confused.

"Something like that," she confirmed, pulling out her phone. "I'll Google it."

"How old was she in *Miss Congeniality*?" he asked.

"That movie's like 15 years old at least," I said.

"We should watch that tonight," Mom said, picking up the remote. "You think it's on Prime?"

"You want to watch *Miss Congeniality* on New Year's?" Dad replied. "That's what we're reduced to? Are we that old?"

"Okay, the internet says she was born in 1964," she said, scrolling on her phone. "She's *way* older than me!"

While they bantered back and forth, Ash and I took a few selfies, gave ourselves the twice-over, and gathered up our coats and purses.

"Thanks for extending curfew," I called to my parents, hand on the doorknob. "I'll be home by 12:30 and not a second later."

"Have fun and be safe driving," Mom said cheerfully, thrilled that I was finally going to Lindsay's party.

"Watch out for wayward boys," Dad added with a wink.

"I think they better watch out for *us*," Ash said under her breath as we left. I stifled a giggle and we got in her car.

CHAPTER 13

We didn't talk much on the ride over, both a little nervous. As we pulled up to Lindsay's house, Ash reached over and squeezed my hand.

"Hey," she said. "I know what you're thinking."

"You do?"

"Yeah. You're worried Harrison is gonna be inside."

I bit my lip.

"Yeah." I hadn't mentioned Harrison much, but I'd been thinking about him nonstop. Like usual.

"Well, don't worry. Because you know what we're gonna do? We're gonna walk in like we own the place. We look amazing, and it's gonna show not only in our clothes but also in our eyes. We're gonna put these assholes on notice. And, more importantly, we're not gonna worry about what any guy—or girl—thinks of us. Because we're only gonna worry about what we think of *them*. And on top of that, we're gonna keep score. *Ist gebongt*?" That's the German way of saying "got it?" and one of Ash's carryovers from Stuttgart.

I nodded and opened the car door. *Here we go*, I thought. My stomach flopped as I stepped out of the car.

When we got inside the house, the party was electric. Lindsay had gone with a white and gold theme in the décor: beads hanging down from the chandeliers, shiny cups in everyone's hands, and dozens, no, hundreds of wall-to-wall balloons.

Despite the glam decorations, almost everyone had come dressed casually. Nearly all of the girls were in skinny jeans—a few in casual dresses, but no one else was in cocktail attire like we were.

And, everyone who saw me and Ash enter the room stopped and stared for at least a few seconds.

Ash was unflappable as always, but I felt a blush starting to creep up my neck. But, I took a deep breath, remembered what I was here for, and looked right back with a Jenner-cool smile.

Just then, Mrs. Wahlstrom tottered into the room with a tray of canapes. She full-on, open-mouthed gaped when she saw Ash and me.

"Oh my *goodness!*" she exclaimed, skittering over to give me air kisses. "Bethany, you look gorgeous!"

"Thanks," I said, fighting not to blush.

"And who's your friend?" she asked, looking at Ash.

"Ash Bauer," she replied. "Nice to meet you."

"And you," said Mrs. Wahlstrom. "I have to say, Miss Ash, I just love your hair."

I saw Lindsay walk into the room with a second tray of apps, clearly seething as she heard her mom.

"I know, right?" Ash said, proudly sweeping a strand back and tucking it behind her ear. I noticed more and more guys in the room subtly turning to look at us, and their gazes lingered. Notably, just like she'd called it, Trevor Chen.

By now, Shane, clearly half a flask in, had moseyed on over to us, hands deep in his pockets.

Hmm, I thought. *Who knew he'd be the first one to practice this on? Especially since he hasn't talked to me in two years.*

He cleared his throat. "Hey, Bethany," he said, and nodded toward Ash. "Hey."

Here goes nothing.

"Hey," I said, looking slightly past him and trying to sound as disinterested as possible (which wasn't all that hard).

"You look really nice tonight," he said, then added, "Both of you."

Five points each. Huh!

"Thanks," I said.

"So, uh, I hear Christian's still in Australia? That true?" he asked, somewhat nervously.

I eyed him curiously.

"That's right."

Shane was quiet for a few seconds, seeming almost relieved. Weird.

"Um. Can I get you something to drink?" he asked, fumbling a bit.

Does this count as a gift? Nah, this falls under chivalry. Two points.

"I'll take a ginger ale," I said.

"Make mine a Coke," Ash added.

"You got it," Shane said, and headed for the kitchen.

Ash gave me a barely perceptible nod and kept typing away on her phone. She was updating his scores already.

It's working.

Just then, Trevor Chen walked into the room and sidled up to Ash.

"Hey, Ash," he said, confidence coming out of his pores as he greeted her with a one-armed hug. "Didn't know you'd be here tonight."

Ash regarded him coolly and slid her phone back in her wristlet.

"Thought I'd stop by," she said, and nodding toward me, added, "This is my friend Bethany."

"Hi," I said easily (and mentally patted myself on the back for keeping my nerves in check).

"We're about to start a game of Cards Against Humanity," he said. "Do you two want to join us?"

"Sure," she said, and I smiled in agreement.

"Great," Trevor replied, flashing a grin. "Come with me. It's going to be in the apartment over the garage."

He then gestured for us to go in front of him. "Ladies first," he added.

Two points.

Once we reached the sliding glass door in the back of the house, he opened it for us and again gestured for us to go out first.

Two more.

Trevor then smoothly linked arms with both of us.

"Wouldn't want you beautiful ladies to slip on the ice out here," he said in explanation, then opened the door to the apartment for us as well.

Hmm. Chivalry and a compliment—seven. He's up to eleven in a span of two minutes—not bad.

We entered the garage loft/Mr. Wahlstrom's mancave to find about a half dozen senior guys setting up the Cards Against Humanity game, with a couple of senior girls perched on the arms of the oversized recliners.

Two of the clearly unattached guys looked up when we came in and scrambled up to offer us their seats on the plush couch.

Two apiece. Guess we better get their names at some point.

One of the girls on the armrest flinched when she saw Ash and me settle into our seats, then looked us up and down before shooting us an icy gaze—which we levelly returned.

Sorry not sorry.

We started the game.

A few minutes in, I was deciding which of my cards would be the best fit for, "Where there's _____, there's ______," (I was gonna go with "Mike Pence" and "an Oedipus Complex"), when the door nudged open. I looked up to see Shane, holding a tumbler of ginger ale in one hand and a tumbler of Coke in the other.

"Hey, I was looking for you," he said, reaching over the heads of some perturbed seniors to hand us our drinks.

"Thank you," I said calmly, placing the cup on a cardboard coaster.

"Thanks," Ash echoed, taking a sip before tossing her pair of cards face down on the coffee table.

Shane stood there expectantly for a moment, then coughed.

"Can I get in?" he asked.

"Game already started," Trevor said, shrugging. "Sorry."

Well, okay. I wasn't gonna fall all over myself for him—that wasn't my new modus operandi, and beside the point since I wasn't interested in him anyhow—but I could still be polite.

"Why don't you be on my team?" I offered.

Shane smiled, saddled up next to me onto the ample arm of the couch—not unlike the other girls functioning as accessories in the room. He hunched over to look at my cards and pointed at the same two I was considering. I smiled in agreement then placed my cards on the table.

A few more rounds passed, and everyone was loosened up from the laughter. I reached over for my cup, took a sip and nearly choked as the sour, pungent liquid burned my throat.

"What's *in* this?" I whispered to Shane.

"Oh. Well, you said you wanted *gin*ger ale, right?" he said with a chuckle.

"Actually, I just wanted regular ginger ale," I said, irritated.

Ash glanced up and quickly typed away on her phone, keeping score. I stifled a smirk.

"Ginger ale? I'll get you one," Trevor said smoothly, and hopped over to the mini fridge to retrieve one for me.

I stole a look back at Ash and she smiled. A few seconds later my phone chirped. I pulled it out to see a text from Ash, reading simply, "13."

He returned seconds later with a fresh can of ginger ale for me but also a replacement can of Coke for Ash as well.

"Thought you might want your beverage tamper-free, too," he said to Ash, handing her the beverage while looking at Shane like he was a toddler caught with an uncapped Sharpie.

Shane reddened, abashed, and muttered an excuse about finding his brother before quickly exiting the room.

After the door closed behind him, Trevor, totally unperturbed, pulled up the next card.

"Ready? Okay. 'I got 99 problems but *blank* ain't one.'"

And I wryly smiled to myself. *Now, where's a card that says "Boys" when I need it?*

I continued thinking that throughout the evening when the other guys in the room were casually flirting with me. One of them was Clay, another senior on the golf team. He was funny and earned himself 10 points by complimenting both my hair and my smile. I was especially impressed that both compliments were from the neck up.

And, as I saw Trevor's gaze linger on Ash and him joke with her in between rounds, I mentally kept scoring him as well. He was at 25 by the time the game had dwindled down, and people started to make their exits for another area of the party.

By then, Trevor was next to Ash on the couch, stealing glances at her long legs, which were stretched out onto the coffee table.

"Hey, I'm gonna head back into the house for a bit," I said to Ash, raising half an eyebrow. "See you soon?"

"For sure," she said.

"Would you like me to walk you back over there?" Trevor offered, standing up.

Twenty-seven!

"No, that's totally unnecessary," I said, waving him away. "Ash, just come and find me whenever you guys mosey over there."

"Will do," she said, clearly comfortable.

I wiggled my fingers at them before leaving and speed-walked through the cold to get back into the house. Now was going to be the bigger challenge. I knew I could do the whole "fake it 'til you make it" thing with my confidence when I had Ash by my side. It was gonna be a lot harder when I had to do it on my own. In a house full of people who weren't enemies exactly, but I sure couldn't call them my friends, and there was a good chance some of them had been talking smack about me that night. Especially Lindsay, whose mom had probably railroaded her into being polite toward me.

Though, whether I felt confident at the moment or not? That was irrelevant, because as soon as I closed the sliding glass door behind me, shook off a shiver, and smoothed down the front of my skirt, the first person I saw, looking at me with an amused grin, from less than ten feet away, was Harrison.

CHAPTER 14

My knees felt weak, my pulse quickened, and I felt myself start to sweat despite the cold. And that's the effect that Harrison had on me even on a normal day.

We hadn't been in touch at all over the past two weeks. I didn't know for sure if he saw me flee the scene after he kissed Mara. He had to know that I knew, though, right? He didn't text me even *once* later that night to see what happened to me and Ash. He never tried to reach me over the entire winter break, and while I wasn't staring at my phone willing it to ping, (*that's a lie, I was)* I definitely noticed his lack of any kind of olive branch or apology.

And, while we went to the dance as friends, you still aren't supposed to kiss someone *else* that night. You just aren't. Especially because if he had half a brain cell working, he'd know that there was at least a *possibility* that I was into him. So, unless he was some kind of low-down, dirty sociopath, Harrison had to have been avoiding me these past weeks out of an overwhelming sense of guilt and shame.

Or, he'd just been busy banging Mara nonstop. Wasn't sure. I didn't see her at the party, though, so maybe not.

All the same, Harrison was no different from any of the guys here (*Yes, he was) (Shut up, Bethany)*, and he had to earn my goodwill, just like any of the rest of them. I was not going to fall all over myself to please him, and moreover, I was not going to brush off that kiss with Mara like he didn't rip my heart out of my chest and stomp on it with his size 12s.

If he wanted my attention, he could work for it.

So, I gathered up my resolve, stared right back at Harrison in the eyes, and then shook my head as if in disappointment. He flinched, clearly taken aback, and I turned to the right to enter the family room, without a word.

I hoped no one could tell that I was practically trembling, and my hands had gone numb. The past five seconds had required every ounce of courage I'd had left in me. I didn't think I could handle it anymore tonight.

But, Ash made her way to the family room, and she flashed a huge grin at me.

"Hey girl!" she hooted, then yanked me over to the larger group, where everyone was on the makeshift dance floor. I started to shimmy a little along with them, laughing and having a good time, shaking off my discomfort of only moments before. As I glanced around my surroundings, I felt how surreal it was. Practically everyone I'd known in sixteen years of living in Snow Ridge was here, and the girls were all just letting themselves go, having fun for the moment, with each other and for each other. Not even noticing the guys, who were all in their side conversations about college bowl games anyway and ignoring the girls back. *This* was how things should be. Everyone was having a blast—for their own sake, and not for anyone else's. And shockingly, I was, too.

And it was then that it hit me.

They have no power over me.

Every last person in this room, in this school, in this town—they could only make me feel inferior if I let them. I had every right to feel worthy and amazing and like I belonged. And I was not going to measure my self-worth by what they thought anymore.

Yes, yes. I know this is what Ash and I had decided when we hit rock bottom the night of the dance. I know this was our goal when we adopted Christian's point system. I know this was the mindset I'd promised to adopt tonight and always. But this was the first time I'd really, truly believed it. Sometimes it takes a while, I guess.

So, about fifteen minutes later, I decided to take a quick break and head into the kitchen in search of a bottle of water, and lo and behold, Harrison was in there, leaning up against the island, fiddling with the tab on his Sprite. He appeared anxious, almost like he'd been waiting for me.

You have no power over me, Harrison, I reminded myself. And this time it came more easily.

"Bethany," he said, voice lowering. "Hey. How've you been."

"Fine," I said, in a clipped, surprised voice. "Why?"

Harrison looked at me, confused.

"Um. I don't know. Just with the way things went a couple of weeks ago."

"What do you mean?" I asked, feigning innocence.

Here it comes. Wait, how many points did we assign for a sincere apology? Oh, that's right, five. Yeah, five would be good.

"You know," he said lowering his voice even further. "How you and Ash never came back to the dance. She must have been in pretty bad shape, huh? Did you guys have to go to the hospital or something?"

I stared at him. Really, of all things, *this* is what he thought happened?

"Noooo," I said, drawing out the word.

"Well, that's good," he said, clearly feeling absolved of any guilt. "I should've texted you to see if you two were okay, but I kinda lost track of time, and then I left for Cabo with my family the next day, so, yeah. Anyhow, is she doing all right? You guys having a good break?" He took a generous swig of his Sprite.

I regarded him, weighing my words. The old Bethany wouldn't even mention the dance and his kiss with Mara, for the sake of keeping up my friendship with Harrison and the hope of one day something more.

But the new Bethany?

Like hell.

I uncapped my water bottle, took a sip, and gently replaced the cap before setting it down on the island next to me. I put my hands on my hips and looked at Harrison with a flat affect.

"Ash and I did make it back to the dance, in fact."

"You did?"

"We did. We got into the fieldhouse and found you. Kissing your ex-girlfriend." And now, my gaze was full of disappointment—in him.

Even with his new Mexico-infused tan, Harrison' face lost all color.

"Oh, my God," he muttered. "You saw that, huh?"

"Yes."

He sighed. "Crap. I'm really sorry, Bethany."

Five points—nah, screw it. Two.

"Sorry you kissed her, or sorry I saw it happen?" I questioned, cocking my head to one side.

Now he looked even more ashamed.

"Both?" he suggested, offering up his hands.

I just shook my head at him.

"Hey, if it makes you feel any better, she's completely ignored me since. She thought she wanted to get back together, but…I guess after seeing me in person, she changed her mind." He looked embarrassed for a second, but then shook his head. "I'm not sure it's over, though."

I wanted to smack him across his devilishly handsome face right there, but instead, I put up a finger to his lips.

"You should probably just stop talking now," I said, then turned on my heels to leave the kitchen.

"Bethany!" he called out behind me.

I turned about halfway around to face him.

"We're good, right?"

I didn't answer. I just turned back around and left the room, on my way to rejoin the girls on the dance floor.

By now, Trevor had joined in with the rest of the dancers, slightly flushed and twirling Ash to the music. As soon as Ash saw me, though, she broke into an even wider grin, and grabbed my hand to playfully bump hips with me.

A few minutes later, Clay, the cutie from the Cards Against Humanity game, wandered into the room. He saw me and beelined over to us and started busting out some moves of his own. Seconds later, we'd all formed a circle around him and were hooting and hollering as Clay made like old school Michael Jackson. I was clapping along, and I couldn't help but notice that he stole a glance at me with each move. And as he moonwalked out of the circle at the end, he tipped his imaginary fedora to me.

"Hey, Lindsay!" Trevor called out, pointing to his watch. "Turn on the TV, it's almost midnight."

Lindsay scurried over to the pile of remotes on the end table, flipped the TV on, and cranked up the volume.

"Okay, everybody," she yelled, cupping her hands around her mouth. "Get ready! It's almost time for the countdown!"

And with just those few words, a blanket of discomfort was tossed onto the crowd. Sure, there were a few girls who were already nuzzling in the corners with their guys, but the vast majority of us were single, sober, and, to be honest, scared of looking like a loser, unwanted. Even with my newfound confidence and badass style.

Lindsay ran into the kitchen and returned with a tray of mini champagne flutes filled with Martinelli's and began passing them around to the crowd. Trever grabbed two and handed one to Ash—and to my surprise, Clay did the same for me.

"Thanks," I said, feeling genuinely surprised and pleased.

Two more for Clay, that makes twelve.

"You're welcome," he said.

Just then, the crowd started to chant:

"*Ten, nine, eight, seven...*"

Clay reached over and took my open hand.

"*Six, five, four...*"

I squeezed his back. Just in front of me, I saw that Trever had his arm around Ash, and her head was nestled under his chin.

"*Three, two, one...happy new year!*"

Clay turned to face me and warmly smiled. I smiled back, both excited and terrified. The only kissing experience I had were those drunken, semi-consensual make-out sessions with Hugh last fall. *Oh, God. What do I do? Do I lean in? Do I close my eyes? Who does what?*

Luckily, I didn't have to think too much about it because Clay simply leaned in and gave me a chaste kiss on the cheek.

"Happy New Year, Bethany," he stage whispered.

I kissed his cheek back and echoed back, "Happy New Year!"

Two more for chivalry. And for just being a good guy when he easily could have been otherwise.

Out of the corner of my eye, I saw Harrison at the border between the family room and the kitchen, stealing a glance at me while pretending to study his fingernails. A smidgen of me wished that it had been Harrison with me in that moment. But even more, I just hoped he noticed me and Clay.

We cheers'd with our glasses, and the tension was broken for everyone in the room as we all began clinking glasses with each other and going on hugging sprees. I didn't see what happened between Ash and Trevor, but I was sure I'd get the rundown once we were in the car.

Speaking of which, we unfortunately had to scoot to make it home in time for our curfew. I found Ash, hugged her, and she asked if I was ready to get going.

"For sure. I'll get our coats from the closet," I offered.

I made my way through the house to retrieve our jackets, and as I returned, I found Ash and Trevor in a corner, her hand in his as he was punching her number into his phone.

He looked up when he was done and looked at Ash like...well, like she was a prize to be won.

"Thank you for an amazing new year's," he said, squeezing her hand. Then, he looked at me, and added. "And thank you, Bethany—it was so good to meet you, too."

He can get two more for that--what a sweetie!

I waved goodbye, Ash and I thanked Mrs. Wahlstrom for hosting such a fun party, and we headed for the door.

"Wait, Bethany!" said a voice.

I spun around.

It was Clay.

"Hey," I said apologetically. "Sorry, I have to jet early. Curfew."

"No doubt," he said, hands in his pockets. "You want to hang out sometime?"

Make him work for it, B, make him work for it.

"Yeah, maybe," I said airily. "You can find me if you try."

"Alright, alright, alright," he said, all Matthew McConaughey. "I will."

I smiled. "Goodnight!"

Game on.

CHAPTER 15

When school started up again a few days later, we brought all of our new attitude and none (or hardly any) of our old baggage with us. For example:

- When we'd sauntered into the commons for lunch on Monday, we took one look at the lunch table we'd occupied in the fall, exchanged a glance, and found Trevor and Clay's table. We were the only juniors but welcomed all the same.
- And then, on Wednesday and Thursday, we sat with Ash's friends from the photography club. A couple of the girls had been at Lindsay's, and we reminisced with them about the party and complimented each others' clothes from that night. I had no idea girls—other than Ash—could be so easy to talk to. Maybe we just needed to have something to talk *about*.
- On Friday, it was an unusual 60 degrees, so we sat outside and enjoyed the sunshine. Curtis, the editor of the school paper, had ambled over, and we found ourselves chatting with him about everything from the keto diet to goat yoga—both of which he was writing about for the next issue of *The Word*. Who knew guys here could talk about something other than themselves?
- Both of us got more compliments than we knew what to do with—Ash mostly for her hot new hair, and me, usually in the form of, "Hey, there's something different about you." I'd generally smile and say thanks, without mentioning that it was likely my new IDGAFWYT approach to Snow Ridge High.

And, of course, all along, Ash and I kept the point system going.

Getting close to Trevor was so easy for Ash it should have been illegal. Only a week in, he'd gone beyond just texting and *called* Ash a couple of times, plus taken her to Red Mango after school on Thursday. He was at 50 points and counting.

Clay had remarkably fewer points than he did—only 19. He hadn't followed me anywhere yet, but he did buy me a brownie at the end of lunch on Monday and saved me a seat Tuesday, where he spent most of lunch getting to know me. I wasn't sure if I liked him yet—definitely didn't dislike him—but I definitely liked that he was working for my attention. Plus, I reasoned, the slower he tallied up the points, that meant the longer I'd get to keep him around.

After talking to Curtis that one day, Ash and I made last-minute appointments with the guidance counselor to switch our schedules so that we could take Media Studies together next semester. Everyone was required to contribute to the newspaper or the yearbook as part of the class, so Ash would be honing her photog skills while I'd be writing articles. The paper was no joke, either—it had won a bunch of awards, and the teacher, Ms. Knox, had been a reporter for the Trib back in the day. Everyone kept an eye out for it each month, and with any luck, I'd get to write some editorials before too long—all part of the plan to get a little notoriety before the next phase of our plan.

But, it pained me to see that, after a week back at school, Harrison was holding steady at the two freaking points earned for his lame apology on New Year's.

Ouch.

When I saw him again in Spanish class, I wondered if he would come and sit next to me again. And oh, he definitely saw me—made eye contact with me, in fact—and raised his eyebrows in greeting before finding an open seat at the very back of the classroom.

Double ouch.

Although, I knew this *shouldn't* hurt—he was the one who wronged *me*, and I shouldn't feel snubbed. If anything, I snubbed *him* pretty clearly at Lindsay's. And it was his responsibility to try to get back in my favor, not the other way around.

Still. I'd clung to the hope that he'd make some kind of effort initially to show me he at least valued our friendship. I thought that he'd extend an olive branch by asking me to partner with him for the next class presentation or offer to buy me a latte by way of apology for his crap behavior the last two times.

He didn't.

Not a single word.

I lamented this to Ash as we drove home from school on Friday.

"Well," she said as diplomatically as she could, "The whole idea of the point system is to help us remain objective and get us to break off contact with a guy before he hurts us. But you're letting Harrison make you feel bad regardless."

"I know," I whined.

"So wouldn't you say that his actions—*inactions*, really—speak for themselves?"

I grumbled something under my breath about the Germans and their damn sensibility, and switched tacks.

"Are you getting together with Trevor this weekend or what?"

"I think so," she said, perking up. "He asked if I'd want to go downtown to go ice skating tomorrow in the city."

"That sounds fun!" I said, trying not to be too envious. Geez, Trevor was gonna make it to 100 in no time flat. I don't think Ash even needed the point system. She just needed to be with a decent guy for once. It was almost too bad we were using him as the control group, and that she'd have to show him the door soon.

"What about you and Clay?" Ash asked, nudging me with her elbow. "You think you guys are on the way to matching hoodies and nicknames?"

"Ha," I said, grimacing at the thought of ever being that nauseating. "No, I mean, I don't know. He's super nice, not to mention adorable, but it's too early to tell. And hey, that's what this system is for, right? To help me stay objective. And ditch him before he gets the idea to ditch me."

"*Das ist gebongt.*"

"Yeah. So you just keep your little matching hoodies comments to yourself, huh, missy?" I teased back, with a hint of truth.

"Yeah, yeah, yeah," she said, pulling into my driveway. "Just saying. Plus, it'd be fun to double date."

"I'll keep that in mind," I said, opening the passenger door. "You still coming over tomorrow night?"

"Yep," she assured me. "We'll be back from Chicago sometime in the afternoon."

"Fab," I said. "See you then!"

The next 24 hours passed uneventfully until about 6 PM when my phone pinged. I thought it was Ash letting me know she was on her way over, but I was wrong—it was Clay.

Clay: CU at the game tonight?

I hesitated before answering. For half a second, my instinct was to text Ash and see if she wanted to change plans and go watch the varsity basketball game tonight instead of our planned *Glow*-a-thon. It *would* be good to have people seeing us out and about with Clay and Trevor, but ughhh, I really couldn't stand going to things like basketball games. Too many people, I hate sports, and plus, I always feel trapped in those bleachers. It's too hard to make an exit.

No, I reminded myself. *Hard to get.* So I decided to play it cas and flirty.

Me: Sorry, Ash and I are having a girl's night. No boys allowed.

He responded almost immediately.

Clay: Rules are made to be broken.

I snickered.

Me: Raincheck?

Clay: K. Maybe a movie next weekend?

Me: Let's talk next week.

Clay: 100.

I then added two points to his column for the text convo.

Just then, I heard my mom padding up the stairs.

"What's so funny?" she asked brightly, nudging into my room with a basket full of clean laundry. "Or who?"

"Oh, no one," I said, putting my phone face down on my bed and grabbing a shirt to fold.

"Ah," she said, folding a pair of jeans and plopping it on my bed. "Male no one?"

"Yes," I said cautiously. "His name's Clay." I didn't want to get too detailed, and I'd already said too much.

"Hmm," she said. She didn't pry any further on him, and instead said, "So how's Harrison? Did he get over that nasty stomach bug?"

"He's okay," I said, shrugging. I'd forgotten that was the lie I'd come up with—I'd told her that he only came to the dance for a few minutes before he came down with explosive diarrhea and had to go home immediately. It explained why I didn't have a single picture with him from that night, plus, I didn't have to admit the humiliation of getting thrown over for Whatsherface.

Mom picked up the empty laundry basket and leaned against my doorframe. "I always thought you two would make a cute—"

Just then, the doorbell rang.

"That'll be Ash," I said, dashing past her and down the stairs.

When I opened the door, she was all smiles.

"Hey," I said in a hushed tone. "So, it went well with Trevor, I take it?"

"Mm hmm," she murmured. "I'll tell you more in a sec."

"I've got a story for you, too," I whispered.

We scampered back up to my room and closed the door behind us.

"You go first," said Ash.

"Clay asked me to hang out next weekend."

"Get out!" Ash said, jaw dropping.

"Right?" I said. "And, like, specific plans, too! He asked if I'd want to go to a movie."

"Look at you go! It's like a …*date.*"

"Maybe. It's a mini-date."

"A datelet."

"I like that. A datelet. So?" I pressed, opening up our Google doc to the Trevor sheet. "Details on *your* datelet today!"

"Okay," she said. "He picked me up at 11, just when he said he would. He had already picked up a vanilla latte for me as a surprise."

"Nice! Okay, he was at 64. We're counting the coffee as a gift of any kind, right?"

"Sure, why not?"

"That brings him to 74. Then what?"

"He opened the car door for me, both when we left and when we got to the parking garage—"

"Okay, four more, so 78."

"Yeah. Oh, and he also told me I 'looked cute in my scarf.'"

"As you do. Five more, 83."

"And it was awesome! We skated around the ribbon for probably about an hour. We each fell down only twice apiece and laughed it off. And toward the end, he took my hand, and we skated that way for a couple of laps."

"Aww!"

"I know," Ash said, blushing. "The whole thing was just *so* sweet. And then we were pretty tired and neither of us had eaten yet, so we walked around to find a restaurant. *And,* he paid for my lunch. The whole time, I don't think we ever had a single drop in the conversation or awkward moment. It's just so easy to be around him."

"You're lucky you found him," I said wistfully.

"For real," she agreed. "And then, we walked around the park a little bit, shared a hot chocolate, and then he took me home. When he dropped me off, we hugged, and it was a long hug. More than normal hug. So then I pulled back, looked at him, and then leaned in and kissed him."

"Aaaah!" I squealed. "How was it?"

"Good!" she said. "Just right, really. Only minimal tongue, and only for a couple of seconds."

"Ugh. I hate you and your perfect datelet," I said, tossing a pillow at her as she batted it away. "Or should I say a for sure *date*?"

"I'd say so," Ash agreed.

"Well, that's 20 points and gives him a total of....oh. Well, that puts him at 103."

That gave us both pause; we both knew exactly what that meant.

"You know," Ash said, slowly. "Whoever said we had to do this exactly like Christian did? I mean, isn't it entirely possible we could, like, *reward* guys for good behavior?"

"Okay, but reward them with what per se?"

This could get sticky, real fast.

Ash pursed her lips. "Or, what do you say we up the limit to 200 before dumping them. Just to give some wiggle room?"

I paused. "This goes against everything we planned, you know."

"It does. But…" her voice trailed off and she looked at me with puppydog eyes.

"Oh my God, fine, I approve," I said, and Ash immediately looked relieved.

"Did you guys talk about plans for the next time?" I added.

"When I said I hadn't seen the newest *Star Wars* movie, he just about had a coronary and promised he'd take me soon. But we didn't solidify anything. I'm thinking we'll text about it and maybe next week figure it out."

"Sounds like a plan," I said, fist-bumping Ash. "Which, ahem, we both have for next weekend."

And what a weekend it would be.

CHAPTER 16

Throughout the next week, I wasn't even thinking about guys for once—I was way too busy studying for finals, which promised to be brutal. I only gave Clay passing thoughts for the most part. And, every time I thought of Harrison, I snapped myself hard on the wrist with my hair elastic, just to try and Pavlov's Dog it.

But, on the Thursday of finals week, Clay texted me to firm up plans. Since Ash and Trevor were already planning to see the new *Star Wars* movie, we all decided to make it a group thing, and Clay and I would join them for the 7:30 show. Ash and I got ready together at her house, chatting a little about the guys, and what was on tap for next week: the first week of the new semester.

"So glad we finally have a class together," she said.

"Same—I think Media Studies will actually be fun, too."

More than that, it could be a good segue onto the school paper, *The Word.* Since my social life had come to a screeching halt freshman year, I'd thrown myself into my schoolwork, but between that and our new plan to rule the school like a couple of praying mantises, I still had plenty of time on my hands. With any luck, the Media Studies class would get me in *The Word,* and we could kick our plan into high gear.

At any rate, I wasn't about to worry about that tonight. Instead, I was going to get my head in the game and see where things might go with Clay.

That week, Trevor had steadily gone up in point value. He called her every day just to say hi—huge in her book—and brought her coffee twice to keep her going while studying. He even met both her parents when he stopped by, too, and mesmerized them for half an hour about his U of C acceptance and plans for the fall.

And true, Clay had texted me a few times that week—nothing major, but I appreciated that he was showing he was still interested all the same. Part of me melted a little over that, but I had to remember, the new me deserved, *expected* basic politeness. The old me would have probably had heart palpitations over it.

Still, I was getting more and more excited for this datelet as the day went on. Plus, with Ash around, there's no way I could have a bad time. I was also interested to see for myself how Trevor acted around her at this point.

"So is he officially your boyfriend now or what?" I asked mischievously as we applied makeup before the guys were due to pick us up.

"I haven't brought it up, and neither has he," Ash said, penciling on her eyeliner. "I want him to be the one to do it."

"He's definitely showing that he likes you, though," I said before blotting my lips. "You could just ask him what's up and save yourself the worrying."

"You and your logic can shut your piehole," Ash joked, giving me a gentle shove.

"Just sayin.' If you're gonna break his heart sooner or later, might be nice to ensure it's in your possession first."

Ash looked like she was about to say something but didn't.

"What?"

"It's—nah, never mind," she said.

"All right," I said lightly. "By the way—are we getting together with your friend Lana next week?"

"Yeah—she said she could definitely get together Wednesday after school. That work for you?"

Ah, yes—bringing us to the previously mentioned phase two. We realized we were getting to a stage in the point system where it was working pretty well, and we thought the time was coming to share it with others. Other girls, that is, and of course only girls who could be trusted not to snitch. You know, like how the first rule of Fight Club is that you don't talk about Fight Club.

We knew we couldn't tell anyone about it online in any way because that would be way too risky—paper trail and all—so it would have to be the old-fashioned way, in person. Ash had a few trusted friends from photography club that she thought would love it as much as we did, so we decided to go from there. Starting with Lana Ogunleye, on Wednesday.

Lana was like a girl version of Trevor, in terms of being well rounded and well liked. She was a senior, in photography club, on student council and the volleyball team. On her mom's side, she was at least third or fourth generation Snow Ridge, but her dad was from Nigeria and rumors were that he was legit royalty. But most importantly, this meant Lana wasn't Snow Ridgey to the bone, and we had a good feeling that she could be both flipped and trusted.

At any rate, it was still Saturday and our guys were about to show up, so that's where our heads were.

"That totally works," I said. "We'll feel her out before anything."

"Obv."

Just then—and promptly on time—Clay pulled into Ash's driveway. Both he and Trevor came to the door, too.

"Evening, ladies," Trevor said with a grin. "You both look stellar tonight."

(Five)

Clay rolled his eyes at him.

"All right, asskisser," he replied. "Ready to go?" he asked Ash and me politely. His car was still running.

"Yep," we said, and headed out. Once the door was safely closed behind us, Trevor put his arm around Ash as we walked to the car.

Clay fell into step alongside me and leaned in.

"You do look really nice, by the way," he murmured so only I could hear.

Five!

"Thanks," I said, a flush creeping up underneath my infinity scarf. "So do you."

And he did look really nice. Clay was rocking a fresh cut, his sandy blond hair wearing it well. He had dark brown eyes, enviably good skin, and a dimple in his right cheek. Clean cut, all-American boy. When comparing him to Harrison (and yes, I realized I needed to stop doing that—easier said than done though), he was definitely just as cute. Plus, charming, funny, and a little bit more mature.

When we got to the theater, the guys paid for us (*ten points each*) and let Ash and me sit together sandwiched between them (*two each for that kindness, too*). About halfway through the movie, Ash had her head resting on Trevor's shoulder, looking like it naturally belonged there. Which, I supposed it did.

Clay had yet to make any move on me. I thought I was putting out the vibe—angling my body toward his, inching a little closer to his seat, and exchanging a couple of laughs with him during the movie's more outlandish parts. But, he didn't seem to be taking any bait.

Come on, I thought. *I know I'm a prize to be won and all, but that doesn't make me a nun, either!*

After the movie ended, we wandered back out into the light of the lobby. Ash and Trevor were holding hands and so tightly bound together they knocked each other's knees as they walked.

"You guys wanna stay out for a while?" Clay asked, stretching into his ski jacket.

I did, for sure. But, the rest of the group was 17 and not susceptible to Snow Ridge's curfew, whereas I still was 16 until June.

"You guys want to come back to my house?" I suggested. "We could order some food and hang out."

Trevor looked at Ash. "Sounds good to me if it sounds good to you," he said to her. (That's worth at least two.)

"Definitely," she agreed.

"Cool, let's go," Clay said, getting his keys out of his pocket. He opened the car door for me when we got to the parking lot too (two).

Once I called my mom and cleared it with her, I'd rattled off my address, and we were on our way.

"You guys want to order a pizza?" Trevor asked, pulling out his phone.

"For sure," said Ash.

"Sweet," Trevor said, and ordered two pizzas by text. When his phone pinged a moment later, he said, "They said they'll be at your house in 45 minutes."

"Great," I said, and we all chatted the rest of the way to my place.

Since Dad was at his monthly poker night, just my mom was in the kitchen when we walked in, reading and pretending she wasn't waiting up for us. I made the introductions, and she chatted up the guys for a couple of minutes before heading up to bed.

"Make yourself at home, everyone," she said, taking her mug of tea and tucking her book under her arm. "Feel free to stick around until midnight."

"Thanks, Mom," I said with a grateful smile. This was new territory for her—me having boys come over—and I was relieved that she was being cool about it, not interrogating them about their parents and their addresses, or whatever. (Who am I kidding? She was going upstairs to text her friends to ask them what they knew. But it was thoughtful of her to *not* make it weird, at least.)

I flipped on the TV, and we all plopped down on the sectional sofa in the family room—Clayton and me companionably next to each other, not too close but not too far, and Trevor and Ash still holding hands. It was all going so well, I couldn't believe it.

Maybe we should abandon the point system and just enjoy this.

An image in my mind floated by of the four of us maybe a decade from now, all coupled together in Ash and Trevor's condo downtown one day, the rocks on Ash's and my left hands glittering under the track lighting as we uncorked a bottle of champagne.

Just then, the doorbell rang and jolted me from my daydream.

"Pizza's here!" I said, getting up from the couch.

Trevor pulled out his wallet from his back pocket and slid out two twenties.

"It's on me," he insisted, handing them to me.

"You sure?" I asked.

Clay, without skipping a beat, pulled his wallet out and tossed a twenty over to Trevor.

"Nah, he and I'll split it," he said.

"Thanks, guys," Ash and I said.

Five each.

The doorbell rang once more.

"Okay, okay," I said, then rushed through the house to the front door.

I pulled it open and lo and behold. Wasn't the pizza guy.

It was Harrison.

"Hey," I said, flabbergasted. "Didn't expect to see you."

"I was out walking Tank, and I don't know, I thought I'd stop by," he said, almost sheepishly. A toy poodle was running circles around his legs and tying Harrison up with his leash in the process.

"Oh."

Was I supposed to give points for this?

The silence started to grow more awkward, considering we hadn't exchanged a word since Lindsay's party.

"Um," he finally said. "I did kinda want to talk to you, Bethany."

My heart started pounding.

Of all times, why now?!

"You did?" I said, clearing my throat.

He looked at his feet, then looked up at me, contrite.

"I've been thinking about what you said at Lindsay's, and I'm sorry. I was a jerk. I never should have been with Mara at all that night, and I definitely shouldn't have blown you off—or Ash."

Every inch of me wanted to melt right then and there. I wanted to throw my arms around him (in all fairness, I usually felt that way around him) and show him just how forgiven he was. But, somehow I kept my act together and bit back all but a small smile.

"Thanks, Harrison," I said sincerely. "That means a lot to me."

And it meant five points for him. I wished it could be more.

"So we're cool then?" he asked.

"Cooler than the other side of the pillow," I replied.

He grinned, then stuffed his hands back in his pockets.

"You having people over?" he asked nonchalantly.

Fack.

"Not like a party or anything," I assured him, blushing. "Just hanging out with Ash and a couple other people."

And of course right then, Clay wandered toward the front door. I saw the expression on Harrison's face immediately transform from affable to grim. I quickly guessed that he remembered seeing me and Clay at midnight on New Year's.

Clay came beside me and put one hand on my shoulder.

"What's up?" he said to Harrison. "Dave, right?"

"Harrison," he flatly corrected him.

"Yeah. Harrison is my, ah, neighbor. He's just out for a walk," I said, pointing at his dog, who by then was trying to gnaw through his leash.

"Well. Don't let us keep you, brah," Clay said, sliding his hand into mine. I think my body temperature rose about ten degrees right there. And then, with his free hand, Clay began to shut the door. Before it closed all the way, I mouthed "bye" and gave Harrison a small wave. His face was stony and silent.

I felt so jittery, so shaken from the last two minutes, and hoped to God that it didn't look as obvious as it felt. Was I glad that Harrison saw Clay with me, to give him a better idea of what he was missing? Or did I feel guilty and mortified for having hurt Harrison' feelings in any way? I didn't know. And the way Clay had acted just then—did I give him points for standing up for me? Or take them away for acting like he *owned* me? It was too gray to figure out just then.

CHAPTER 17

The new school year began on Monday, and along with it, the new me and Ash were in full swing. And, as no one but the two of us expected, our stock rose at an unprecedented rate.

Have you ever heard the saying, "dress for the job you want, not the one you have?" Well, we were going to be the HBICs of our own lives, and, we'd decided that with our new attitudes, we'd continue to kick our style up a notch. We started watching YouTube videos to master a dozen ways to wear a scarf. Heels for school, because why the heck not?

Now, let me remind you, Snow Ridge takes the word "conform" to a whole new level. Yes, the girls wear clothes that could be considered on trend, just like at any high school, but unlike any other high school, "Goodwill" was a dirty word. Snow Ridge's unofficial uniform consisted of approximately four brands. On any given day, I'd see two girls wearing a duplicate shirt in a class, shooting each other surreptitious dirty looks. (Well, what did you expect, sweetheart? They'd discontinue it just because you bought it?)

People at Snow Ridge High definitely took notice of our new looks, just like they had at Lindsay's party. But I think it had much more to do with the way we carried ourselves, too. Confidence begets confidence, and after that past weekend of feeling like a total boss, it carried over to Monday. We sauntered into school, laughing and feeling like a million bucks. About twice as many people as usual said hi to us, looked up from their phones as we passed them in the hallway, and I just felt seriously *alive* for 7 AM on a Monday.

Media Studies was the first period of the day, so doubly awesome—Ash and I not only had the class together, but we got to hang out from the car ride to school until second period. As we headed into the newspaper office, where class would be held, we casually took our seats at the large conference table that substituted for desks. We were slinging our bags on the backs of the chairs when I heard a surprised voice.

"Hey, I didn't know you'd be here!"

I looked up, and there was Curtis. I remembered how he'd been super easy to talk to that day Ash introduced me to him at lunch and broke into a smile. He had toast-brown curls, was about five-foot-ten, weighed maybe a buck thirty soaking wet, and wore a faded Weezer tee, jeans, and an easygoing smile.

"Heeeey!" Ash said in greeting, reaching for a hug. "Well, after you trying to recruit the photography club to *The Word* all year, I figured I may as well get some class credit for it."

That, and we were going to use The Word to our advantage, if we had anything to say about it.

"Good call," he said amiably. He then looked at me. "Hey, you're Bethany, right?"

"That's me," I said good naturedly.

Curtis slid into the seat next to Ash as more people filed into the class. Nearly everyone greeted him as they arrived—it made sense that everyone would know him, since he'd taken this class multiple times as a de facto study hall for *The Word* editors. The other editors taking the class, Wes, Arthi, and Joe, introduced themselves to us, and we were all immediately chatting like we'd been friends for ages.

Then, just as the bell ring, the last person to drag her navy Hunters into class was Lindsay.

Great, I thought glumly. *Can't wait to see her smug face every morning.*

Then, I snapped out of it. *Who cares? She can suck it.*

My second thought was a lot more accurate as Lindsay saw Ash and me sitting with the seniors in the room like we belonged there. She slightly grimaced and found a spare seat on the far opposite end of the table.

Then the teacher, Ms. Knox, came in, bearing two large boxes of Dunkin Donuts in her arms.

"Morning," she said brightly, tossing the boxes on the table, along with a small stack of papers. "Feel free to help yourselves, and make sure you grab a syllabus."

I noticed that everyone took a donut, except for Lindsay.

Though Ms. Knox did make a point to smile in her direction and say, "Miss Wahlstrom! Glad you're joining us. Getting into the family business?"

Ah. I'd almost forgotten to mention that her dad owned Wahlstrom Printing Company, right here in Snow Ridge (est. 1917). They printed the local newspaper, the village magazine, and, donated their printing services for *The Word* as well.

She just smiled politely and noncommittally as usual.

I went back to scanning through the syllabus and saw that Curtis was listed at the top as Teaching Assistant. Seriously? You could do that as a student?

I looked over at him, and he was hunched forward, absently doodling on his napkin.

"Curtis, you're up. Can you give your spiel on *The Word*?" Ms. Knox asked right then, rubbing a hand through her thick white hair.

"Sure," Curtis said, still doodling but now looking out at the class instead. "So, the paper comes out the first Thursday of every month, and as you've seen, gets distributed in the commons, plus you get an e-version to your school e-mail. We have two features, at least two and up to three op-ed pieces, and humor columns, news, sports, and entertainment, and you'll all get a chance to write for it all this semester. You'll sign up for a different section each month, and we"—he gestured to himself, Arthi, Wes, and Joe—" will work with you on how to write in *The Word* style.

"And," he added, looking around the room at each person while somehow still doodling, "We're going to give credit where credit is due. You write an amazing article or submit a great photo, and we'll publish it. Simple as that. We're always looking for talent, and hey, it'll give you a little more cred, or at the very least, a couple more followers."

I'm counting on it, I thought, smiling a little.

"Thanks, Curtis," Ms. Knox said, taking over again. "As you see on the syllabus, your first assignment is to write an op-ed piece. Contrary to what you might think, the name doesn't come from 'opinion-editorial'—it's because the placement in a traditional paper is *opposite* the editorial page. But it is an opinion piece all the same.

"In *The Word*, we've titled that op-ed spot 'Tell Me What You Really Think.' And as such, I want to know what *you* really think. Whether it's about a school policy, or a human rights issue, or something related to a global event—make a compelling argument for why you're right and why your plan of action makes sense. You're going to be less judged on the opinion itself, and far more on how you make a case for it.

"300 words, due Thursday."

Ash and I glanced at each other and grinned. This was right up our alley. Everyone else around the room was nodding thoughtfully, except for Lindsay, whose normally composed face was darkening by the moment. Not surprising, though—she lived by her reputation and likely wasn't keen on sharing her *true* feelings with the world.

I was kicking myself for not having signed up for this class earlier. Ms. Knox was frigging *awesome*! I'd never had a teacher like her, who talked to us like we were adults, and for that matter, cared what we *really* thought.

The bell rang, and everyone jumped into action, stuffing syllabi into binders and grabbing their bags.

"See you tomorrow, guys," Ash said, looking at the editors.

"Bye," I echoed.

"See you ladies," Curtis said, and stood up. He then handed me the napkin on which he'd been doodling all morning. I peered at it and furrowed my brows. It was a caricature—and a flattering one, at that—of me and Ash, back to back, standing in *The Word's* office, posed like the old *Buffy the Vampire Slayer* posters, only we were wielding pens and notepads. The caption read "Word Slayers."

I gaped at him.

"Oh man, I love it!" I said, completely impressed.

"Welcome to *The Word*," he said, and strolled out of the room.

Ten! Even if he was my sort-of teacher.

CHAPTER 18

A couple weeks into the semester, and things couldn't have been going any better for me. I'd improved my social standing with the snap of a finger (or rather, with the discovery of Christian's spreadsheet), my classes were totally manageable, and I felt like I was glowing. Ash and I had never felt more confident and we were totally unstoppable.

So much so, that Ash and I did, in fact, start the Snow Ridge Female Empowerment Club.

We went back and forth on the idea—a lot, in fact—but ultimately, what had changed our mind was when we got together with Lana.

Ash and I had met up with her at Starbucks to hang out/secretly gauge her that first Wednesday of the new semester. She was super-friendly, and we were bonding over our shared love of bad reality TV and, to my surprise, equally shared love of *The Handmaid's Tale*. That was a good sign.

"So," she said to me, taking a sip of coffee. "I hear your brother's in Australia now?"

"Yeah," I said. "He alleges that he's volunteering with Habitat for six months in Brisbane, but in reality, he's there for the year-round surfing and Foster's on tap. He's such a fraud."

There, I'd said it. Now, her reaction would be key.

"Ugh," she said, rolling her eyes. "My parents are letting my brother study abroad in South Africa right now because he was all 'I want to explore my history.' Yeah, first of all, we're *Nigerian*, and second of all, I can guarantee you that all he wants to explore is what's underneath South African panties."

Well, then.

"So unfair, right?" I said sympathetically.

"Totally! If I had the chance to go abroad, I would make every second count," Lana said, clearly irritated. "But since he's getting to go, they're not going to drop that kind of dime on me too. Or my sister Kaia, for that matter."

"You know," Ash said smoothly, "I feel like guys around here get their way most of the time. Don't you?"

"Please," scoffed Lana. "It's all the time."

"Someone should do something about that," I said.

"Well, there's strength in numbers," Lana said. "I'm glad you guys see it clearly. I thought I was the only one."

"You're definitely not," Ash said.

"We should form a club," I said, grinning at Ash.

And with that, the Snow Ridge Female Empowerment Club was off to its unofficial start. Being a senior, Lana was already super busy and couldn't commit to the actual launching of it, but she said she'd for sure come to the meetings if Ash and I got it off the ground. And Ash and I talked about it on the way home and realized that this truly was the next logical step if we wanted to take down the Snow Ridge patriarchy. Our overarching goal wasn't just to keep score of the guys in our life (though that sure was fun and empowering in its own way); it was to change Snow Ridge and take a few whacks at its plexiglass ceiling.

Next up was getting a faculty advisor, and the obvious choice was Ms. Knox. We asked her the very next morning.

"Of course I'll do it!" she said, clapping her hands and letting out a whoop.

"This won't be a problem with you being the student advisor for *The Word*, right?" I asked, just to cover our bases.

"Not for a nanosecond," she insisted. "In fact, I think it goes hand in hand perfectly. At *The Word*, we stand for freedom of speech. In a feminism club, you stand for equal rights. What could be more important?"

We grinned.

"Thanks so much," Ash said. "We'll put together the application."

"Perfect," Ms. Knox chirped. "Only caveat is you'll also have to present this to Dean Dean, but I can't see that he'd have any objection."

Ash froze, remembering Homecoming weekend like a 'Nam flashback.

"I'll present our case to Dean Dean," I said, hoping Ms. Knox didn't notice Ash starting to tremble, and we swiftly exited the classroom.

"You okay?" I asked, squeezing her arm.

"Ugh," she replied.

I didn't blame her. Ever since Homecoming weekend, when Seamus Dean had spread all those ugly rumors about Ash, she blanched anytime she saw either him or his dad in the hallways. And God's honest truth, Dean Dean sneered just a little every time he saw her, too. Ash would never have cause to be sent to his office, with her grades and behavior both outstanding, but she sure as hell kept her nose extra clean to avoid ever being in a room alone with him. I knew what kind of trauma having a one-on-one with this guy for the purpose of starting a female empowerment club would have on her. I saw the irony, sure, but I didn't think it was funny at all.

"Like I said, I'll handle Dean Dean. I got you," I promised.

And a week later, there I sat in his office as he poured over our application, clearing his throat and keeping his face as blank as possible. Finally, he leaned back in his chair and crossed his arms.

"A 'female empowerment club,' hmm?" he asked.

"Yes," I replied, smiling proudly.

"And Ms. Knox has agreed to oversee it."

I grinned. "So, as you see, we filled everything out. Can we start one?"

He hesitated a moment before speaking.

"We strive to keep all things equal here in Snow Ridge, Bethany."

HAHAHAHAHA! I thought, fighting to keep my face placid. *Sorry, go on.*

He continued, "We can't prevent you from starting a female empowerment club. In the same way that we couldn't prevent a student from starting a male empowerment club."

He said that. He really, really said that. But it was just us in his office, and I had no witnesses. Like so much in Snow Ridge, it was behind closed doors.

I took a deep breath. "Do males here feel not empowered?"

He kept his affect flat.

"I'm stating facts to you, administrator to student," he said blandly. "So that you have all the information available when you make your position."

I felt myself starting to sweat, but I couldn't stop myself. I just couldn't. And moreover, I *wouldn't.*

"We have an African-American Student Association, a Latin-American Student Association and an Asian-American Student Association," I said, trying to keep my voice level. "Are you saying that the school would, or wouldn't, approve a European-American Student Association? In the case that the European-American students needed a safe space to feel empowered?"

And that was what did it. I saw a tinge of red creep up his neck and the tiniest flash in his eyes. He leaned forward, scribbled his signature on the final page of the application, and slid it back across the desk.

"Tell your dad I'll see him at paddle," he said with a withering look.

After I closed his office door behind me, I run-walked as fast as I could back toward Media Studies. I hadn't felt so exhilarated and scared since...well, since I'd ask Harrison to the winter dance. But I'd done it!

That night at dinner, I was halfway through my pork chop when my dad said out of nowhere, "Well, I got an interesting phone call from Mr. Dean today, Bethany."

Record scratch.

"Word travels fast," I muttered. "Was he calling as my dean or as your racquetball buddy?"

He gave me a wry smile.

"I think he was mostly calling me as a fellow concerned father," he said.

"Oh, please," I retorted. "Concerned that I'm going to teach my female classmates how to voice opinions?"

"What's this?" my mom asked, setting down her fork and knife and folding her hands together on her lap.

"Bethany here has decided to start some kind of girls-only society," Dad replied, stabbing his pork chop with his fork.

"It's a female empowerment club," I explained. "Where we'll talk about real issues, and how to fight for equality. Women's rights are human's rights, you know. Like Hillary said."

He slightly choked, then recovered by taking a long drink of water.

"I would think you'd be glad that I took the initiative to launch a club," I added. "College applications are like, eight months away. I've got to get something on it other than a high GPA."

"There is that, Gary," Mom said evenly.

He looked at her much the way that Dean Squared had looked at me earlier.

"There is that," he said flatly. "Just don't expect me to buy you a Subaru."

I wrinkled my nose. "Huh?"

"Never mind."

So I might not have won over my dad, but my mom was happy that I was happy, and that counted for something. And then, a few more sprinkles were added to the sundae.

CHAPTER 19

When I walked into Media Studies the first Thursday of February, Ms. Knox was already in class waiting with stacks of *The Word.* Being in her class, we got the perk of early distribution.

Once the bell rang, Ms. Knox stood in the front of the room, looking anxiously excited. The rest of us, barring *The Word* editors, were a little confused but patiently waiting.

"You've had three assignments so far, and, as you know, certain articles that have proven to be just truly exceptional—well-written, thought-provoking, and reminiscent of *The Word* style—are considered for publication each month," explained Ms. Knox, reiterating what Curtis had told us a few weeks before. "I'm thrilled to say that there were two standout articles from this class that we've included for the February edition in the 'Tell Me What You Really Think' slots."

She turned on the smart board and linked to the first article.

Please, please, please be mine, I hoped.

"We have an op-ed on the importance, and disappointing lack of, FAFSA preparation and education at Snow Ridge High School, by Lauren Kissel," Ms. Knox proudly announced.

We all politely applauded and high-fived Lauren as Ms. Knox read the article aloud, taking time to annunciate the occasional line for dramatic effect.

"And, for our second article," said Ms. Knox, fiddling with the smartboard as she pulled up the next one, "is a piece by Bethany Cummings, on the sexism and body-shaming inherent in the administration's ban on leggings."

Bam!

When I was researching the school handbook on how to start the feminist club, I'd noticed a few other things in there. One of them was that there was an addendum to the dress code this year, insisting that leggings were only to be worn under skirts and dresses. Last semester, I'd immediately complied, relinquishing them all to the back of my closet in fear that I'd ever be mistaken for walking a fine line with school policy.

But, since coming back this January, I'd shopped my closet and realized I had a few leggings that I'd like to wear again without hiding them under extra yards of fabric. I figured I couldn't be the only girl in Snow Ridge annoyed by this new rule—there had to be a pantload who agreed with me. Thus:

Not Without My Leggings
By Bethany Cummings

The Snow Ridge High School dress code had one major change this year. If you're a girl, you may have had to make several changes to your wardrobe. If you're a guy, you probably didn't notice at all.

According to the dress code, "leggings are to be worn only under shorts, dresses and skirts. Anyone not in compliance will be sent home with an unexcused absence."

Wait, wait, wait. Now, the administration is getting involved in the "are leggings pants?" debate, at the expense of female students' rights?

According to the dictionary, "pants" are defined as "a piece of clothing usually reaching from the waist to the ankle and covering each leg separately." I'm pretty sure that leggings (not to mention tights, long underwear and some Spanx) fall into this category.

Moreover, we deserve an honest answer as to why exactly this rule has been put into place. I shouldn't have to camouflage my rear's outline just because the school is worried I'll distract the boys—instead, the boys should treat girls like human beings, and not objects to look at for their own entertainment. (Or, if they do stare at us, are we supposed to believe we were "just asking for it?")

This rule seems symptomatic of a double standard in society, and yes, in Snow Ridge itself. Boys are encouraged to walk around shirtless at

> the school-sanctioned football games, painting the letters to spell "Snow Ridge" on their chests in packs of nine, while girls could be covered in fabric from head to toe and still face suspension.
>
> I wonder what would happen if a guy wore leggings to school as a joke one day. Would everyone laugh along with him—or would he be sent home unexcused?
>
> We deserve fairness in a dress code, or no dress code at all.

And as Ms. Knox read each sentence, I felt more and more conviction in my opinion. I peeked at my classmates, and the girls were vigorously nodding while the guys' emotions ranged from irritated to chastised. Curtis, though, caught me looking at him, looked at me like he was proud, and shot me a thumbs up. Ash gave me a squeeze and whispered, "You are freaking amazing, B!"

As class ended, I grabbed a couple extra copies and lingered a moment until it was just Curtis, Ms. Knox, and myself left in the room.

"Nice work," Curtis said. "And by the way, it was unanimous among the staff when we read it. We loved the way you called the administration flat out on the sexism issue."

"Thanks," I said, grinning.

"Always refreshing to see a student unafraid to shake up the system a little," Ms. Knox agreed. "Recognizing hypocrisy. It'll be a good talking point when the club launches tomorrow."

I couldn't wait. Though, there was one thing nagging at me.

"Ah, is there any way I'm gonna get in actual trouble for this?" I asked, a little less confidently. I knew that if Dean Dean didn't hate me before, he definitely would now.

"Absolutely not," insisted Ms. Knox. "We believe in freedom of the press, and furthermore, you made a more than valid argument. And, if anyone will get reprimanded, it'll be me," she added with a wink. "I've fought battles a lot bigger than this one."

I had no doubt. Ms. Knox marched to her own drummer in Snow Ridge, and she quite likely relished these opportunities. She was already my perfect ally.

"Okay, then," I said, relieved. And, at any rate, what was done was done. No turning back now.

As Curtis and I walked out of the classroom together, he gave me an extra copy of the issue.

"Keep this one," he said with a smile, then headed down the stairs.

I opened it up and flipped to the third page where I found my article. He'd sketched a picture next to it to mimic the Netflix landing page for "Narcos," although instead of Pablo Escobar surrounded by cash and kilo bags, it was a picture of me, and the caption "Leggings" underneath. In that picture, I had a slightly evil, but definitely all-powerful, grin and stacks of folded leggings were all around me.

I chuckled. Just call me Bethany Escobar.

To be fair, Curtis was as amazing a guy as I could have ever hoped to meet, but I wasn't really thinking of him in that way. First of all, he was practically my teacher. Second of all, I was still keeping tabs on Clay's points (he had yet to break 75, let alone 100). And third of all, I didn't know how well-matched Curtis and I would be. As self-assured as I felt most of the time these days, he was still so different from me—intellectual, offbeat, and more grown up, really—and I didn't know what we'd have in common. And lastly, he was going to school in Michigan six months from now, so why even worry about him?

Ash called me out on it.

"You're thinking of not thinking of Curtis," Ash insisted, when I lingered over his feature on the opioid crisis at lunch.

"Am not."

"Uh huh."

Though, to be even fairer, I didn't find myself thinking too much about *any* guy—rather, I was focusing on myself and what was best for me. Unlike last semester, Ash and I weren't spending hours on end analyzing every little thing guys would say to us or dissecting every text to figure out their hidden meaning. We just entered their scores and moved on to the next to-do item of the day. Romantic? No. Practical and sanity-saving? Yes and yes.

Shockingly, this practicality even applied to Harrison. (Mostly. Except for the days he didn't shave and had that sexy stubble going. Then all bets were off.) And his lack of action in my direction made me a bit more receptive to Clay's steady gains. In fact, a few days ago Clay had asked me to go with him to the Planetarium soon as an extra credit outing for his Astronomy class (datelet!). I'd felt a little thrill and let the lights dim on Harrison a bit more.

I'd felt buoyed by the positive response I'd gotten all day from my article—rumor had it that it was going to be an agenda item up for review at the next school board meeting!—and I decided I would ask Ms. Knox if I could join *The Word* as a staff writer.

The next morning, I dawdled once again after class to corner Curtis and Ms. Knox about the idea. After I broached the subject and made a brief case for myself, the two of them exchanged an amused glance.

"Funny you should mention this now," said Ms. Knox. "I was actually going to ask if you might be interested in writing a monthly column for us."

"That would be perfect!"

"Have you seen the online version of your last column?" Ms. Knox asked. "You've gotten more than 200 comments. I don't think any column has sparked this much interest or controversy in a while. Plus, you're a sharp writer. We think you've got it in you to do something like this every month."

"Well, thank you!" I said, delighted. "I'd love that."

"Great," Ms. Knox said approvingly. "The official staff meeting is every Monday right after school. Why don't you come next week?"

"I'm there," I said, typing it into my phone calendar.

"And, a lot of us are here after school most afternoons, anyway," added Curtis. "You're welcome whenever. Some people like to get their writing done here, others send it in. Either way's fine."

"Got it," I said, scooping up my bag. "I'll be there."

"And I'll see you in the library for the club launch today at 3," Ms. Knox confirmed.

"Club launch?" Curtis asked.

"Female Empowerment Club," Ms. Knox said. "Ash and Bethany are starting it."

Curtis raised his eyebrows and nodded approvingly.

"Right on," he said and smiled. "You'll rock it."

Ash and I met in the library at 3, both of us a little nervous. Mom once admitted to me that she hated hosting parties because the first 15 minutes of them were always so unbearable, always wondering if anyone was gonna show up. But to Ash's and my delight, show up they did.

Including us and Ms. Knox, we had nine of us there for our first meeting. Nine! We thought that was impressive—especially in Snow Ridge, where the term "feminist" was a slur. There were some girls Ash recruited from Photography Club, two sophomores named Ella and Cristina that I didn't know yet, and true to her word, Lana, along with her sophomore sister, Kaia.

We started off with an icebreaker of two truths and a lie. Mine were "I'm an avid reader; I'm a Cancer; I failed my first driving test." (I'll let you guess which one was the lie.) Ms. Knox was relishing this, though. Hers were "I marched against Nixon and the Vietnam War; I'm a past president of the Snow Ridge Township League of Women Voters; I'm a flat-Earth truther."

And then, we went around the table and summed up in one sentence apiece why we came to the club that day:

"Because I think girls need to have a stronger voice."

"I thought I was the only one who realized this town was stuck in the 1950s."

"Because I see #NotAllMen posted a lot more than I see someone willing to post #MeToo here."

And it was so clear, to all of us, that we were in the right place—with the exception of Kaia, Lana's little sister, who sat there sulking with her arms crossed, much like I used to at Christian's soccer games. I didn't sweat it when she begged off for cheer practice after about 20 minutes.

We decided we'd meet every two weeks, and before the next meeting, we'd each come armed with one or two ideas of what we'd like to accomplish in the club over the next year.

We were off to a great start, and the rest of the week passed like normal. Then, on Friday afternoon, I was vegging on the couch, thinking about what my next column should be about—our school's ridiculous new abstinence-only unit in Health class? Or questioning our school's obsession with contact sports in light of everything we're learning about CTE?—when my phone rang.

For the second time in two months, it was Ash, crying.

"It's over," she said.

CHAPTER 20

"What's over?" I asked.

"Trevor and I are," she said, sniffling. I held the phone back from my ear, wincing as she blew her nose.

My heart dropped.

"I don't get it—what happened?"

"We were hanging out at my house after school, and he was being kind of quiet and I don't know, just *off.* So I asked him what was wrong and he's all, 'nothing.' And then I go back to watching *TRL* and then after a while he finally says, 'Well, I guess there's something.'"

"Oh, great. What'd he say?"

"I looked at him, like, 'All right, I'm waiting,' and he started to look a little nervous. Then he took a deep breath and said, 'I just think the whole.... Female Empowerment Club' – and he used air quotes around it, mind you—'is a little. I don't know. It's a little...much.'"

"Really."

"And he said that his friends were giving him crap and asked him if he was gonna join, too."

"Well, we don't have any rules against it," I said dryly. "We'd certainly let him in if he wanted to further the cause."

"He also admitted that his friends were joking about me being a lesbian, saying my haircut all made sense now. And then he asked me if I would consider *growing out my hair again.*"

"Wow, first of all, using 'lesbian' as an insult? What year do they think this is?"

"It's not what year it is—it's what town we're in," she said, irritated. "So I got really pissed, and I thought about his points. I know, I know, I kinda abandoned the whole dump him at 200 thing, and I should have done it before we got to this argument. But I just went ahead and told him we were through."

"You dumped him, just like that?"

"I did. I steeled myself, told him that coldly as I could, and added that he should probably leave right now. It's not only that he thinks 'lesbian' is an insult, though that's pretty eye-opening. It's that he thinks 'feminist' is an insult, too. He's done."

"Wow," I murmured. "So, how do you feel?"

"At least I waited until he left to start crying like an idiot," she said, tearing up again. "Ugh. I thought our new plan was supposed to keep me from feeling like utter crap. If I'm the one in control of my life, why do I feel like I just lost something so perfect?"

I didn't know what to say to that. She already knew she screwed up the system by not dumping him earlier—I didn't need to remind her of that.

"Well," I finally offered. "Maybe if you had just been passive and sweet when he said that, it would have started him going down a slippery slope. It starts with the language he uses toward you. Maybe he would have started treating you like garbage in other ways. At least this kept you from going through any of that before it happened?"

"Or," she said emphatically, "What if I just completely overreacted, and I just dumped him over nothing? Should I really have just kicked him to the curb over that?"

"What's that phrase— 'when people show you who they are, believe them?'"

"But," she countered, "Is *that* how he showed me who he is? Or was it the 99 percent of the time when he treated me like a queen? Which am I supposed to believe?"

I hesitated, then said, "I don't know. But. Back to the point. What do you think Christian would have done in your shoes?"

We both thought for a moment.

"He would have dumped him—her, I mean—whatever—without a second thought," she admitted. "And if he's anything like you say, he would have a new girlfriend by dinnertime."

"At any rate," I said, "I think it's a lesson learned. We do the dumping right when the guy breaks 100. Worked for Christian, apparently."

"I know," Ash admitted. "I just wish it didn't have to suck so much."

And, unfortunately, suck it did. Because what I hadn't realized was how closely tethered my burgeoning relationship with Clay was to Ash and Trevor's temporarily strong one.

The next morning was Saturday, when Clay and I were supposed to go to the Planetarium. We hadn't firmed up whether we'd drive in or take the train, and I texted him for the details. An hour passed by, and nothing.

Mildly annoyed, I resorted to calling him. After two rings, it went to voicemail—which you *know* means that he saw me calling, and then slid me to his voicemail box. Which you *know* no one ever checks.

Another hour went by, with growing more and more irritated by the minute. I texted one more time "?" and in news that will shock no one, he didn't reply to that either. Instead of on a date downtown with the guy I *thought* was practically my boyfriend, I spent the day sulking on the couch, eating pretzels, and rereading *Outlander*. (Though I kept finding myself jealous of a fictional character. Claire never had to deal with this shit from Jamie.)

When I went back to school on Monday, I tried looking for him in the commons, where he usually grabbed breakfast before school started. Wasn't there. I caught a glimpse of him in the parking lot after school—and I know he saw me—but he quickly hopped in his car and pulled out of the lot with a screech.

Jackass.

And it hit me like a punch in the gut that just like Ash and Trevor's relationship, ours was over, too. The second punch came at the realization that Clay never liked me that much either, and as a part of me had feared, he *had* been just taking one for the team all along. And, just like Trevor and every other guy in Snow Ridge, he equated feminist with threat.

I felt sick. I felt used. I guarantee I felt like every girl on Christian's list that he'd dumped. And I felt utterly helpless about it.

I didn't want to go back to my old, desperate ways to try and get his attention. Clay and I also had never added any kind of official title to our relationship, so it's not like I was in a position to dump him per se. In effect, he was just flat-out going to ghost me—with Valentine's Day coming up, no less—and the worst thing about it was that he was going to get away with it.

Check it, no. There was *one* worse thing about all this. I was in the *exact same place* that I was the night of the dance two months ago. Everyone in school was going to know I'd just been ditched and laugh about it behind my back. I'd just been cast aside like a chicken wing with half the meat left on it. And I was furious.

This was *not* what Ash and I had in mind when we set up our grand master plan. The idea was to keep *us* in charge and prevent this kind of godawful treatment before it happened. We were better than this. We were going to take the guys at this school down a notch, come hell or high water. It then dawned on me what my next column for *The Word* would be about.

"Bethany?"

I whirled around in my chair in *The Word*'s office.

"What's up, Curtis?"

He frowned and cleared his throat.

"I read your column," he started. "And it's…um…"

"Yes?"

"Well, it's definitely opinionated."

"You got that right," I confirmed, then narrowed my eyes at him. "Why? Something wrong with that?"

He scratched his head and sat on the edge of the conference table, studying a printout of my first draft. He removed the red pen tucked behind his ears, made a few notes, and handed it back to me.

"I'm the last one who's gonna try and censor you. I'm just confirming it's what you want published."

"Never been surer of anything in my life," I said smoothly. "Other than my love for vanilla lattes, sleeping late, and *Empire*."

"I think you could teach Cookie Lyon a thing or two," Curtis assured me, tucking the pen back behind his ear with a smirk.

Class is in goddamn session, I thought.

A few weeks later, if there was anyone at Snow Ridge High who hadn't known my name yet—well, they sure would know it now:

"Why Ghosting Doesn't Work,
You Morons"
By Bethany Cummings

Ladies, raise your hand if this has happened to you. You've been seeing a guy, and everything's going better than you could have ever hoped. You laugh at each other's jokes. You feel butterflies when you're around him. You love learning all there is to know about him, and simultaneously feel like you've known him your whole life. Life couldn't be sweeter or savorier.

Then, all of a sudden, *poof!* He attempts to disappear from your life. He puts the kibosh on healthy routine you've created of texts, calls and time together, without a word of warning. He avoids you in the hallways. Even your mutual friends remain in his custody.

He's ghosted you. And you're left wondering what's wrong with you, where you went wrong. *Why did this happen to you?*

Well, don't.

There's nothing wrong with you. And *everything* is wrong with him.

First of all, I'm no mathemagician, but I can tell you that in a school the size of Snow Ridge High, the odds of him running into you again—in class, at lunch or, I don't know, *walking around*—are pretty darn high. What kind of idiot thinks he can suddenly become selectively invisible?

Second of all, what does he really think he's proving by doing this? That he's better than you? If he believes that, he is sorely mistaken. The only thing he's proven is that he's immature, afraid of confrontation, and would rather run away than face the music. Good luck functioning in the real world as an actual human, buddy.

You're worth more than that. You're not only a prize to be won (and, if you ever doubted this, *please know it is true!)*; you also deserve to be treated with respect at every stage of your relationship: beginning, middle, and yes, the end.

Don't waste a second feeling sorry for yourself. Instead, feel sorry for the next girl stuck with him and his cowardly rear end in the future. And be glad it isn't you."

After seeing the final version of it just before the print run, I felt more than a little trepidation—despite what I'd told Curtis. What if this backfires? And what was I thinking, admitting that I'd been ghosted—is anyone else going to admit it happened to them, too? And what if Clay tries to exact some sort of revenge on me over this? Ugh. Maybe this was a big mistake.

"You know, Bethany," he said quietly. "I think you're brave for doing this."

I chewed my bottom lip and then let out a mirthful laugh.

"Brave or stupid?" I asked.

"There's always a fine line, isn't there?" he said sardonically. "But you fall on the brave side. No question. And what was it that Ned Stark said right off the bat in *Game of Thrones*? Something like, 'The only time you can be brave is when you're afraid.'"

I raised an eyebrow at him.

"You think I'm afraid?" I asked, putting a hand on one hip. "Of what?"

"Isn't everyone afraid of putting themselves out there for the judgment of everyone else?" he responded matter-of-factly.

"People do it all the time," I scoffed. "C'mon, everyone posts more selfies than anything else."

Curtis gave me a knowing look. "With filters."

"Well, yeah, with filters," I conceded.

"And you know that there's a huge difference between sharing who you are on the outside versus who you are on the inside," he insisted. "Don't get me wrong, I know you're Snow Ridge's answer to Tiffany Haddish *and* Elizabeth Warren, but it's only natural to worry about what people think of you from time to time. I know I do, anyway."

I couldn't have been any more surprised when he admitted that.

"Curtis, your act is so together I don't think you could pry it apart with a chainsaw. You're the head of the paper, everyone likes you, and you're going to an amazing college next year. How could *you* possibly worry about people judging you?"

After a beat just too long, he replied, "Didn't say I worried about what *everyone* thought of me. Just certain people," he added softly.

I felt my heart start to beat a little faster. And he was so close I could smell the fresh lemon laundry scent coming off his Gorillaz shirt. He smelled like a cozy afternoon in bed.

Wait. No. Bethany, just no. Bad idea.

"So," I said brusquely, clearing my throat and taking a step backward. "This looks good to me. No typos. You think it's clear for print?"

"You got it," he said.

I took a deep breath. "All right," I said. "I'll keep an eye out for it next week. Come what may."

"Come what may," he agreed.

And then—I didn't really see it coming. Any of it.

CHAPTER 21

The morning the next issue of *The Word* was released, my article had been greeted with laughs and applause in Media Studies class.

The girls in this town were going to have their voices heard if I had anything to say about it.

But not everyone was as excited about it as I was.

When my article came out during the first lunch period of the day, I was still in Physics. My pod and I were still reading over our lab instructions when the secretary from Dean Squared's office slipped into the classroom and whispered something to Ms. Gray.

My teacher frowned and then looked in my direction.

"Bethany, can you come here, please?"

I felt that mini-heart attack feeling that you only feel when you can't find your phone.

I slowly stood up and walked over to the front of the room, noting the side-eyes from my classmates as they pretended to read over their labs.

"Bethany," Ms. Gray said quietly. "You've been called to the dean's office. Mrs. Melvani will escort you there."

"Oh, um, okay," I said, completely flustered. "Should I leave my stuff here, or…?" my voice trailed off.

"You better bring it," Mrs. Melvani said with her solemn lilt.

"Okay." I scooted back to my pod, knocking over my stool on the way, muttering an apology to my lab partners, and hightailed it out of the room.

The walk to the dean's office was technically a quick one, but it seemed to last a lifetime. When Mrs. Melvani opened the door, I looked up and saw a dangerously calm Dean Squared sitting at his desk. And, across from him, was an equally unruffled Ms. Knox.

Here goes, I thought.

"Sit," the dean directed me, and I obediently jumped into the open vinyl chair next to Ms. Knox. Dean Squared stared at me, somewhat curiously, as if he were deciding what to make of me. He drummed his fingers on his desk, then let out a slow, coffee-tinged breath.

I waited for either one of them to speak, my heart banging like a gong.

"Miss Cummings," he stated.

"Yes."

"I read your column this morning."

"Excellent, wasn't it?" said Ms. Knox proudly. "She's a fine addition to *The Word*." She looked at me and pointedly smiled.

Thank goodness she was in my corner.

"'Excellent' is hardly the word I'd use," sneered Dean Squared. "I'd call it sarcastic, misanthropic, and absolutely uncalled for. I'd call it an embarrassment to our school. Moreover, it's borderline bullying, and as you know, we strictly enforce a zero-tolerance policy toward—"

"Now, just wait a minute," interrupted Ms. Knox, holding up a hand. "That's over the line. There's absolutely nothing wrong with that article—"

"The headline includes the word 'moron,' in it. That's absolutely meant as an affront to one of our students, and furthermore…"

I couldn't even make out what the two of them were arguing about anymore as their voices continued to rise over each other. All I could think about were the words "embarrassment" and "bullying" racing through my head, and I tried my hardest not to throw up or start crying right then and there.

That wasn't what I meant at all. I was just telling it like it is. I wrote it to stand up for myself about how I deserved to be treated. And sure, maybe to throw a little shade at Clay for being a jerk, but actual bullying? I wasn't a bully!

Was I?

"Is that clear, Miss Cummings?"

I shook myself out of my own head.

"I'm sorry, can you repeat that, please?" I asked meekly.

Dean Squared looked at me sternly. "You, along with the staff of *The Word*, are on warning. If I see even a hint of an insult against another student, the paper will cease to publish for the remainder of the school year. Not only that, any students or staff members involved will be punished accordingly. Is that clear?"

As he'd continued to speak, his gaze had left mine and traveled over to Ms. Knox's, where the two of them stared, transfixed, neither willing to blink first. Then, Ms. Knox broke into a wide smile.

"Crystal clear," she said cheerfully. "Now, may we be excused? I'm certain that Bethany here needs to get back to class."

Just then, the bell rang, signaling my lunch period. I wasn't about to correct her.

Stony-faced, Dean Squared nodded toward the door, effectively dismissing us. When the door was solidly closed behind us, and the din of the chattering in the hallway could camouflage the shakiness in my voice, I let out a deep breath.

"I'm so sorry, Ms. Knox," I said woefully, again trying to hold back my tears.

She looked at me with a hint of mischief.

"You have absolutely nothing to be sorry for," she insisted. "Between you and me, he's probably just sore about your last article leading to the board reevaluating their dress code decision, and there was nothing he could do about it."

"Really?" I was uncertain. And a little surprised that even someone as anti-establishment as Ms. Knox would say that out loud—she *was* still a teacher.

"That, and a month doesn't go by without me getting called in there. It's like state cops with their quotas for pulling cars over," she said, half-joking.

"Still, I don't think I want to be on Dean S-…Dean's radar," I admitted. "I've never been sent to the dean's office once my whole life."

"And look what you got sent for!" she said proudly. "Standing up for young women who deserve better treatment. Of all things, that can't be the worst, can it?"

True. But in equal amounts, it was also about publicly embarrassing Clay.

"Um, well, no, I guess not. Though I would still rather not get sent to his office at all."

We'd reached the commons area and I paused, now that I was at my destination. I looked all around and saw everyone with their copies of *The Word* and suddenly felt another wave of anxiety wash over me.

"Bethany, you just keep doing what you're doing," Ms. Knox said, looking me in the eyes. "I've got your back." She started humming and ambled toward the stairwell. And that was that.

I went into the lunchroom and sat by myself for a moment, again paralyzed by the thought that I'd be ostracized after this article. Maybe everyone would think I was bullying Clay, too. And maybe they'd be right.

But, only seconds later, Lana—who'd started designing our Female Empowerment Club t-shirt logo last week with an amazing "Don't FEC With Us" tagline-- slid right next to me, open-mouthed and eyes gleaming devilishly. She thwacked me with her copy of *The Word.*

"Bethany, you are *bad*!" she said, laughing.

"You think so?" I asked, trying to sound casual.

"Only in the best way possible," Lana replied. "Dang. That was perfect. You straight up *exposed* Clay."

"Ah, so it was that obvious that it was about Clay, huh?" I said, feeling myself start to sweat again.

"So what?" she said, shrugging. "He's a big boy. He can take it. Plus, it needed to be said. He's hardly the only dude here who's tried that nonsense. Seamus Dean did the same thing to me when I was a freshman. Dirtbag."

I wondered if she knew what he'd done to Ash. Certainly wasn't my place to tell her, though.

"I personally love it that you got back at him," she added. "If only every girl had a way to do that."

It was time.

"Hey," I said, lowering my voice. "Can you keep a secret?"

She looked intrigued.

"About what?"

"Well," I said. "It all started when my brother gave me his old Macbook for Christmas…"

Between that conversation, and my article, I couldn't concentrate at school all day. I couldn't help myself—during each passing period, I whipped out my phone to scan the comments of the online version. Lots were pretty positive:

"It's about time someone said that!"

"This happened to me, too. She's dead on."

"Thank you for the reminder. I am worth more than that."

"LOL mathemagician"

Though, there were some comments that stung—not because they were cruel (those I just skipped over), but because they were like little truth vaccines jabbing me without any anesthetic.

"She complains about being dumped. Well, you reap what you sow."

"When does the guy she's talking about get a chance to voice his side?"

"I'd like to know what exactly makes her a 'prize to be won.' Not being sarcastic, just wondering."

"If that's how she talked to her ex, I can see why he'd disappear on her!"

I was looking down at my phone on the way to Spanish when someone sidled up next to me and hissed in my ear, "Loved your article."

I snapped my head up. It was Clay, glaring at me.

"You," I breathed, experiencing about the hundredth internal emotional meltdown of the day. Though it occurred to me that this was the first time he'd approached me since the last time he'd kissed me, and I hadn't forgiven nor forgotten. So, screw any guilty feelings at the moment.

"I guess now you remember who I am?" I said sarcastically.

He narrowed his eyes at me and crossed his arms.

"That was pretty low, you know."

"Really?" I said, getting defensive. "Lower than you completely blowing me off? Lower than you acting like you cared about me, then ghosting me?"

"That's not the point," he growled.

"That's exactly the point," I said back to him, my voice getting louder. "And, it's not like I even used your name. You can't even claim it's libel."

(I was right about that at least. I looked "libel" up before we went to print.)

A few people had stopped to look at us. Noting this, Clay shoved his hands in his pockets and looked at me like I was a hair in his food.

"Whatever," he muttered and stomped off down the hallway.

I physically shook myself off, leaned back against a locker and glanced around. Everyone was back to minding their own business. Good. I'd had enough of this day. I pulled my water bottle out of my bag and took a quick swig to calm myself down more. I was screwing the cap back on when I felt a tap on my shoulder. I jumped and let out a yelp.

"Whoa, sorry!" Harrison said, backing away.

"Whew, it's just you," I said. "Sorry. Not *just* you. It's—never mind. I've had a day. What's up?"

Harrison smiled the way only he can.

"I read your article today."

"Yeah?" I said wearily. "What'd you think?"

He made a slight bowing motion toward me.

"It was good! Though, I feel like I should make it clear that I will never, ever ghost you, Bethany."

"Thanks," I said warily, as we walked into the classroom and took a seat. "Good to know."

Of course, already emotionally wrung out for the day, this made me wonder what he meant by that. Was this a sign that he liked me? A compliment? Or, as Ash would think, another coin in the slot machine? Five points? Gah. My head was too scrambled to sort it all out.

"Yeah, 'cause I'm pretty sure the next time someone does that to you, you're gonna go straight for the jugular. And I like having my neck attached to my head," he added with a grin.

I playfully(ish) punched him in the arm. A few times.

"Ow," he laughed melodramatically. "Back off, *lucha libre*!"

“You really think guys are afraid of me now?” I asked. “For real.”

“Only if they know what’s good for them.”

Before I could stop the words from coming out of my mouth, I said, “But do *you* know what’s good for you?”

He looked at me curiously and opened his mouth as if to say something. Then the bell rang, and the moment, whatever potential it had, was over.

CHAPTER 22

After school, I rushed out to the parking lot to find Ash. I couldn't wait to get out of that building.

"Go, go, go," I practically yelled once we were both inside her car.

"Dude, what happened?" she asked, looking at me like I had two heads.

"Just the most insane day ever," I moaned, and filled her in on my day.

"Holy…," Ash said and let out a low whistle. "What a roller coaster."

"You're telling me," I said. "I can't believe it's only Monday, either."

"No kidding," she said. "Speaking of which, guess what I got treated to seeing in the hallway today?"

"What?"

"Trevor strolling into the commons with his arm draped all over Lindsay like last year's poncho."

"He didn't!" I exclaimed, gaping at her.

"Yup."

"When did they…?"

"Don't know. But any thoughts I had about apologizing to him or trying to work things out have been effectively flushed down the toilet," she said glumly. "And to think I just dumped him like two weeks ago. Stupid of me, right?"

"Oh, Ash," I said sympathetically. "Trevor sucks. He does *not* deserve you. Seriously, don't even waste your time being sad about this loser. Just concentrate on the other things we've got going on, you know? By the way, club secretary—what's on the agenda for the meeting this week?" I added, hoping to distract her, and me.

"Let me think a minute," she said squinting. "Yes. Okay, Lana's supposed to present the t-shirt designs. Ali is gonna finalize the petition for turning the Spring Fling into the school's first-ever turnabout dance, so that girls asking guys will be the norm. And, Ms. Knox is looking into school guidelines to see if we can do that Women's March photo art installation we talked about."

"Nice!" I said. And it really was. Our numbers had doubled to nearly 20 in just a month, and I had a feeling that even more people might show up to this week's meeting.

"You know, Ash," I said. "We should be proud of ourselves. And even though the point system didn't exactly work as planned—*yet*—I'm sure it's gonna pay off soon."

I didn't mention that I'd shared it with Lana, though.

Ash looked over at me and gave me a wan smile.

"About that," she started. "I don't know. I'm starting to think our whole…point system…it's not such a great idea."

"What?!"

"Well, look at where we are. It hasn't exactly improved our love lives, you know," she said. "I just don't know that it's worth the trouble, you know?"

"Of course it's worth it!" I bellowed. "It was what gave us the motivation to change our life in the first place. Which, in turn, has made this an overall amazing semester for us. We're rocking *The Word.* We started FEC. We're more confident—"

"Maybe *you're* more confident," she retorted. "I feel like such a damn loser now that everyone knows Trevor and I are over—and for the record, everyone believes that *he* dumped *me.* It's almost worse than after that whole debacle with Dane Alexander, to see him fawning all over Lindsay. Seriously, B, this kinda sucks. I should look into graduating early."

"Ash!" I said aghast. "Just give it time! You'll get over him. And besides, we're gonna flip this school on its head, and it's not a question of if but when. I mean, come on. We already are."

Ash didn't look convinced.

"*Ist gebongt,*" she said offhandedly.

To break the tension, I said, "I think this day calls for some cookies. You want to come over for a bit and bake with me?"

"Definitely."

We pulled into my driveway and saw something—or someone, that is—totally unexpected at the curb, dragging enormous suitcases out of a taxi.

"The hell are you doing here?" I asked, slamming the car door shut behind me.

"Hi to you too, B," said an extremely bronze Christian, swinging a frame backpack over his broad shoulders.

"No, really," I said, folding my arms. "I thought you were gonna be in Australia another week."

"My Great Barrier Reef tour got cancelled on account of a cyclone in the area. So I switched my tickets and came back early, thought I'd surprise Mom."

"Hey," Ash piped up, padding over to us.

I saw Christian's eyes slightly widen, and he straightened his posture

Pssh. Dream on, douchebag.

"This is my friend Ash," I said, gesturing toward her.

He beamed at her, flashing his toothpaste-commercial smile, offset by his turbo-tan.

Barf.

"I'm Christian," he said. "Bethany's big bro." He tried to put an arm around me, but I recoiled. Clearly, he thought he could fool her into believing that he and I were loving siblings. Again, dream on!

"Yeah, I know," she said lightly. "I've heard… so much about you."

"Well," he said, again with that fake-ass grin, "I'm gonna be in town for a minute before I start college. So if you need anything, just let me know."

"Ash, we should probably go to your house so that Christian and my Mom can have their joyful reunion," I suggested.

"Oh, good thinking," Ash said, giving Christian a quick eyebrow raise as a "nice to meetcha," and headed back toward the car.

"Don't leave your shit everywhere inside," I said to Christian. He didn't hear me—he was too busy watching Ash walk away.

Once we were back in the car, Ash said, "He didn't seem like that big of a jerk."

I rolled my eyes.

"Do you not remember that he *invented* the point system? He's like, the devil incarnate when it comes to girls."

She half-frowned. "Well. It's not like I'm planning to find out for myself."

I snorted. "Exactly. Anyway, let's go bake. And figure out the rest of the agenda."

"You got it, sister."

CHAPTER 23

After school the next day, Ash and I both headed to *The Word* office. Curtis and I were copy editing the news briefs, and Ash was working with Wes on the layout for the recap on the school musical. Ash had recently taken photos from the audience and backstage, and there were enough good ones to do a "Noises Off"-themed photo essay.

Ms. Knox happened by their workstation and marveled over the idea. She was in a great mood, as usual, and when Ash and I were getting ready to leave, she beckoned Ash over.

"I'll go warm up the car," I offered, and she tossed me her keys.

About five minutes later, Ash joined me in the car, grinning excitedly.

"Guess what?" she shrieked. Then, not bothering to wait for guesses, she said, "I have my first photography job!"

I let out a whoop.

"Get out! Where? For who?"

"Ms. Knox's brother is a wedding photographer, and he needs a third shooter for a wedding down in Naperville on Friday night," she said, as she maneuvered onto the road. "He asked Ms. Knox if she had any promising students she could recommend, and she said she first thought of me!"

"Well, obviously!"

She smiled triumphantly. "Don't get me wrong, it only pays $9 an hour, and I'll be mostly there to lug around his camera bags. But he said that if it worked out, I could probably do more weddings! And the season's only just starting."

As it did turn out, Ash was an exceptional third shooter (I'm biased, but I think she probably could have been a first shooter) and started getting booked for weddings nearly every weekend. Which meant that I'd be seeing less of her—but that was okay. I was keeping busy.

My mom lent me her car to go to Lana's "little get-together" on Friday, which turned out to be maybe seventy of her closest friends from the senior and junior class. Most of the usual suspects were there—Clay, Trevor, and their friends, who gave me sour-faced scowls in greeting and would have gladly spiked my drink with rat poison if I'd ever set it down.

But it wasn't just those types who were at the party. Lana was someone who transcended cliques and was genuinely friends with all kinds of people. Though, they all had *something* about them. As I glanced around the room, it crossed my mind that they were the kind of people with a spark inside them that you can't put your finger on, but you know is there all the same.

And then, another thought occurred me: *Maybe it's not just the Christians and Lindsays of the world. Maybe we've* all *got that fuse—it's just that some of them get lit sooner.*

I heard someone strumming a guitar in the den and wandered in there to investigate.

"Curtis!" I exclaimed. I don't think I'd ever seen him outside the Snow Ridge High building and grounds.

He stopped mid-song, and his face lit up when he saw me.

"Hey, c'mon over!" he said, waving me toward the small group by him. They were some of the seniors from Madrigals, all a little flushed and together, trying to eke out an acoustic version of "My Shot" from *Hamilton*. At some point we pulled up the lyrics on someone's phone to try and sing along, but we were hilariously bad.

The singers went to refresh their drinks, leaving me and Curtis alone.

"I hadn't expected to see you here," I said smiling. "Didn't know you ventured out at night."

"Well, all work and no play makes Jack—or Curtis—a dull boy."

"*The Shining*—nice. Okay, which do you prefer: book or movie?"

He thought for a second. "Well. Both are good. *But*, when it comes down to it, I'm gonna choose the book, every time."

"Me, too," I said with a grin.

Just then I heard my name.

I spun around to see Lana, waving me over to a group of people in the kitchen nook.

"Be right back," I promised Curtis before going to greet Lana for a hug.

"Hey, hon," she said, giving me an air kiss. "You girls know Bethany? This is Sarah, Lesley, Colleen," Lana added, pointing out each one around the table.

The girls were all seniors, and I barely knew them. But, they all greeted me with bear hugs and knowing looks, which was pretty weird considering. Despite that, it felt *so good* to have this group of people automatically greet me like I was someone worth knowing. Instead of like someone they'd find a way to excuse themselves out of a conversation with.

"Bethany here is the one who's been writing those hilarious articles in *The Word*," Lana said with a wink.

One of the girls, Sarah, widened her eyes in remembrance.

"Oh my gosh!" Sarah said. "I wanted to tell you. The one on dumbass guys who try to ghost you? That was freaking *hilarious.*"

"Yes!" agreed Lesley. "Although I really liked that one you wrote on leggings. Talk about a double standard. You nailed it."

"Thanks," I said earnestly, flattered that anyone would have remembered. "It looks like the school board'll change the dress code for next year, too."

We made more small talk for a while, and before we all went to our separate areas of the party, each girl gave me another massive hug again and put her number in my phone.

This was nice…but something was up.

After a while, I pulled Lana aside. "So—a lot of these girls here are kinda acting like they know me. Like really well."

"Well, they admire you, that's for sure."

I paused. "Did you tell them? About the point system."

Lana winked.

"It's not a bad thing," she said. "Just, you know. *Observe* tonight."

I did look around, and I saw that every girl in a conversation with a guy had her phone in hand. I watched one pair, who I recognized as Dani Watson and Arthur Cook, flirting over in the corner of the kitchen. I surreptitiously spied on them for a few minutes, laughing and Arthur leaning over to brush a blonde strand of hair out of her eyes. When he left for a moment to refill her drink, she pulled up a spreadsheet on her phone, made some quick notes, and shoved the phone into her back pocket before he returned.

Well, that looked positive at least.

Then I looked over and saw Seamus Dean and Jenna Quentin.

Ugh. Why was he even here? I bet Lana didn't invite him, but he showed up anyway.

What was also troubling was knowing that Jenna was a really sweet girl. She was super gorgeous but super shy. Passive. Not one to make waves. She and I had partnered up for projects a lot in middle school, actually. And knowing enough about her, I knew that she could easily be Seamus's next victim.

I watched them out of the corner of my eye. And I saw something in Jenna. He was laying it on pretty thick, but she looked…skeptical. He had an arm around her, and when it drifted down lower and lower until he quickly made the move and cupped her ass…her eyes flashed, and she threw his arm off her, stomping off in disgust. He looked bewildered, and quickly looked around to see who saw. My eyes innocently shot back down to my phone.

"Dyke," he muttered, then went to refill his beer.

I found myself sneaking out of the room to find Jenna, and she was in the hallway outside the bathroom. Angrily punching in statistics onto her phone.

I grinned.

Not worth it, Ash? This was 100 percent worth it.

And you know what else was worth seeing over the next month? The female revolution at Snow Ridge High.

CHAPTER 24

I may have just provided the matches, but these girls—nope, young *women*—around me were the fire. FEC had grown to 30 members and climbing. Our petition to turn the Spring Dance into a turnabout had gained 200 signatures, and with that, Student Council had voted to make the change for the following school year. And when I walked the halls, there was a select contingent of females who grinned and winked as they passed me in the hallways—and a similar-size contingent of guys who found themselves dumped for the first time.

And they were *pissed*. You could feel the anger and their feelings of injustice radiating off of them. Fights were breaking out in the hallways weekly, with guys all circling and egging them on, as the girls in the know tried to hide their smirks. One guy even punched a wall, leaving aftermath of a dent and a broken hand. The less self-destructive guys were spending extra time in the weight room after school, working off the sexual frustration and humiliation.

I know you're not supposed to take joy in other people's pain. But you know what? I reasoned that the girls had experienced a lot of that same kind of pain in the first place.

The only thing really missing in all this was Ash.

She was MIA a lot. Other than dutifully taking minutes at FEC, I'd noticed with more than a little sadness that Ash had abandoned our whole plan entirely. So, I decided to have a come-to-Jesus talk with her about it. I waited until after school on a Friday to approach Ash.

"Ash," I blurted out, once we'd fallen into a lull in our normal conversation in the car. "I feel like you've kinda left me hanging here."

"What? Why? Is it because I'm so busy working now?"

"It's not that exactly," I clarified. "I feel like we were on a roll earlier this semester, and we were really going somewhere, and now it's like you're…gone somehow. C'mon, dismantling the patriarchy would be a lot more fun with your help," I nudged.

She sighed. "That whole plan was misguided. I was just mad at Matt. Don't you think it's just all about revenge? I don't know about you, but I'm over him. And Trevor."

"It's about more than revenge," I insisted. "It's about giving girls here a voice for the first time. Don't you think that's worth it?"

"Well, yeah. And FEC is probably the best thing we've ever done. But the whole point system has made me feel…icky. Especially knowing that so many girls are using it."

Lana had told Ash that she knew about it a couple weeks ago. Ash had been horrified. And pissed at me. Really pissed.

"I don't know why you don't see its value," I lamented. "Think of all the amazing things that's happened and the confidence we gained from it. Look at us! You're a professional photographer. I'm a professional writer, kind of. For the first time, girls in Snow Ridge are standing up for themselves. They're dumping guys before they get hurt. And—"

"I'm not going to keep having this argument with you," she said, exasperated. "I've moved on from that stupid idea, and I think you should, too. And I *really* don't think you should have advertised it to anyone else, especially not without talking to me first."

I fell silent.

"Hey," Ash said quietly. "You're my best friend, and always will be. And if you want to lead the Snow Ridge feminist crusade, then I'll back you up. But Bethany? Just let this point system go."

"Well," I muttered. "I'll think about it."

We were quiet for another couple of painfully long minutes. Finally Ash spoke up.

"So, I met a guy."

My head whipped around toward her.

"You *what?* Who? Where? Why have you not told me this before? Details!"

"His name is CJ. I met him at a Chipotle after I shot a wedding two weeks ago, and because I wasn't sure what I thought about him," she answered, smiling. "But the more I get to know him, the more I like him."

"He picked you up in a Chipotle," I mused. "I don't know what I'd think of that, either."

"There's a lot more to him than that," she insisted. "He's in college. He's super sweet, really funny, and we've been texting a lot since I met him. After I shoot an engagement photo session in Oswego tomorrow, I'm meeting up with him. He's taking me out to dinner. Not at Chipotle, though," she added with a wry smile.

"Ash Bauer, look at you," I said approvingly. Though, I added as a bestie should, "If he starts treating you badly—he's a dead man."

"*Ist gebongt*," she said, then squeezed my hand. "All right. So how are things in the guy department for you? Any updates? How's Harrison these days?"

"I was afraid you would ask that," I admitted.

"Why?"

I sighed. The truth was, I still wasn't over him. As badass as I tried to be these days, whenever he shot me the right smile in Spanish class or popped by my house when he was walking Tank, he wrapped me just a little tighter around his finger. And deep down, I knew that no point system would, or could, keep my feelings for him in check.

"Because I just can't shake him from my head. He'll be normal-friendly, cordial, for weeks, and then he'll say something flirty or pay me a really sweet compliment. And I'll think we're sharing a moment and finally getting somewhere, and then he goes back to being just normal-friendly again."

"Slot-machine," Ash said in a sing-song voice.

"Ugh. Shut it, Bauer," I said.

"You know who would never do that to you, though."

"What? Who?"

"Curtis. Obviously."

I felt myself redden. "He's not into me."

"Oh, please."

"I'm serious. For starters, he hasn't shown any romantic interest in me. He's never even texted me once. We're basically coworkers," I said, ticking the points off on my fingers. "I mean, he is a great guy, don't get me wrong. He's helped me a ton, he's made me enough comics to fill a book, and the things he says to me are so—so *thoughtful*."

"Exactly. I don't see the problem here," Ash said. "Sounds like he wants to become friends with you and get to know you first."

"He probably *only* sees me as a friend. Otherwise, don't you think he would have made a move that was, well, more obviously a *move*?"

"He's in a tricky position," Ash said, "He's the editor of *The Word*, and he's also Ms. Knox's assistant teacher, or whatever the heck he is. I bet he thinks it's inappropriate to make a move on you."

"It probably is inappropriate."

"And the bigger thing is—you're leading the frigging feminist revolution. He would never, ever want to offend you, and probably has no idea *how* to make a move on you. You've burned the old rulebook, but you haven't written the new rules yet."

"Oh my God," I mumbled. "You're totally right." I hadn't considered any of that.

"As per usual," she said with a wink. "The real question is, when it comes right down to it, would you want Curtis to make a move on you?"

I'd put off asking myself this for as long as I could, but now that Ash had voiced it, I let myself truly think it through.

"Well…I mean, of course I would, hypothetically," I said slowly. "He's super-intelligent, funny, easy to get along with. I can't think of a single thing I dislike about him. And, he's cute, not gonna lie."

"Then go for it," Ash said. "Ask him out."

"Me?"

"You have to!" she argued. "You're the one who keeps saying you're so confident and in charge of your life."

"All right, fine," I muttered. "Do I have to do it today? I can't do it today. I'll do it Monday. Or some other time next week."

Or maybe she'll forget about it, and I won't have to go through the excruciatingly painful process of asking a guy out.

"Monday," she cheerfully ordered. "And don't think I'm gonna forget about it, either. And do *not* even think of collecting points on him, okay?"

I sighed.

"Okay. Monday."

CHAPTER 25

The worst thing about knowing you have to do something scary on a Monday is having the entire weekend beforehand to stress about it. And make no mistake, the prospect of asking Curtis out was terrifying.

I'd texted Ash all weekend in an effort to weasel my way out of it, too:

Me: *He's probably too busy to hang out with me. AP tests are coming up.*

Ash: *So ask him to get dinner as a study break. Everybody's gotta eat.*

Me: *I'm gonna look like an idiot if he says no.*

Ash: *He won't say no. Plus, he's graduating in two months and you'll never have to see him again.*

Me: *If he liked me, he would have made a move.*

Ash: *No offense, the guys who *have* made a move on you treated you like something they'd scrape off their shoe. Go out and get him. Life is short.*

I stuck around after school in *The Word* office on Monday, "working on my article." Ash had purposely left so that I'd have to ask someone for a ride home—with any luck, that someone would be Curtis.

One by one, the other editors and staffers had wiggled into their jackets, tossed their cans of Diet Coke in the bin, and shuffled their way out of the office. Around five, even Ms. Knox had put on her moto jacket and helmet, citing dinner plans with her "beau." And then, half an hour later, it was just me, Curtis, and the sports editor, Joe, who was wrestling with Illustrator on the corner computer.

I was staring blankly at the screen. I'd barely written anything, far too worried about my task at hand to concentrate on my next column. Which, as it so happened, had to be a big one for me. This would be my last "Tell Me What You Really Think" piece before the end of the year, so I had to make it count. It had to be a crowd-rallier, something all the girls in Snow Ridge could get behind. But what?

"You're here late," Curtis said from behind me. "Writer's block?"

I swiveled around in my chair and squinched my eyes shut.

"Yeah," I groaned. "Could say that."

He clucked sympathetically.

"Been there," he said.

Just then, his stomach let out an audible grumble.

"Well, it's official, I've been here too long, too," he said apologetically. "I'm not gonna get anything else done tonight."

Now or never, B.

I cleared my throat. "You wanna grab something to eat?" I asked, my voice raising half an octave.

His eyebrows furrowed and he looked at his watch.

"Um," he said.

I hurriedly backpedaled, "It's okay, you don't have to—"

"No, no, that sounds good. I just have to be somewhere by 7."

"Okay," I said, now feeling not only uncomfortable, but like an imposition. "If you're sure."

He grinned. "Definitely. You okay with closing up shop, Joe?"

He muttered something unintelligible at the computer and waved us off. That seemed good enough, so we left Joe to his own devices and wandered out to the parking lot toward Curtis' Prius.

"I should probably mention that you also need to chauffeur me wherever we go," I apologized.

"No worries," he said, opening the passenger door for me (!). "I know you usually hitch a ride with Ash, but I'm happy to do it."

"Thanks," I murmured, sliding into the car before he closed the door behind me.

After a quick discussion, we decided on Portillo's. It was one of the ones with a lot of movie props and posters, so we sat under the replica biplane.

"So," he said, once we'd gotten situated. "Let's not talk shop."

"Okay," I said, with a smile small (*datelet? Twenty points? No, no, stop it, Bethany. Just enjoy it.*).

"What's your favorite guilty pleasure TV show?"

Part of me was surprised Curtis actually watched TV.

"Hmm," I said, thinking. "Probably *Bachelor* and all its offshoots. You?"

"*House Hunters International.*"

I almost spit out my water.

"What are you, like 70?" I teased.

"It's the greatest show *ever*," he said, totally unperturbed. "The best is seeing the internal scream face on the realtor whenever the clueless American says they want a place with 'rustic, Old-World charm," but they want like six bathrooms and all stainless appliances. For $500 a month."

"'Internal scream face,'" I repeated smiling. "I thought I was the only one who noticed that on people."

Curtis grinned, framed by his toast-brown curls around his face.

"I notice it all the time," he said earnestly. "Besides, people always say more silently than they do aloud, don't you think?"

I swallowed hard. "They sure do."

We chatted for another half hour without a single lull in conversation until Curtis checked his watch again.

"Shoot," he said. "I've got about 10 minutes to make it to the library." He did some quick mental math, realizing that he wouldn't have time to take me home.

"I can come with you," I offered. "I'll just ask my mom to pick me up from there."

"Okay," he said, visibly relieved. "Or, better yet, why don't you come with me to club?"

"Club?" I asked warily. "What kind of club? Model train club? Stamp club? Book club?"

He smiled. "C'mon. You'll love it."

So, ten minutes later, I found myself outside a small conference room at the Snow Ridge Public Library.

"Actually, can you hang out here for just a couple of minutes?" he asked. "I've gotta prep them for you."

"Okay," I agreed, feeling more confused and intrigued by the minute.

Curtis darted into the room and quickly closed the door behind him. I couldn't make out any of the words, but I heard him and a few other voices murmuring through the door. A moment later, he ducked back out.

"I think we're good," he said, smiling and reaching out for my hand. "Come on in."

We entered through the door, and there was one petite adult woman and a group of five boys, all looking around middle school age. They all seemed a bit anxious, one drumming his pencil nervously on the table.

"Guys, I'd like you to meet Bethany," Curtis said, slowly and clearly. "She's a friend, and she's here to draw with us tonight. Can you say hello to Bethany?"

"Hi," most of them said quietly. One continued to perseverate in the corner, twirling his hair.

"Thanks for joining us, Bethany," the woman said warmly, coming over to shake my hand. "I'm Ms. Atwater—I'm the occupational therapist-slash-facilitator. Curtis does all the real work, though," she added, grinning at him.

Curtis looked a little embarrassed but quickly clasped his hands together and cleared his throat.

"Okay," he said, addressing the room. "After last week's vote, we decided that we're working on superheroes this week, right? Anyone have a favorite?"

"Batman," one called out.

"Deadpool," yelled another.

As each one shouted out, Curtis wrote the suggestions furiously on the dry erase board.

The boy who'd been quiet in the corner typed something into his iPad then wandered up to the front of the room to show Curtis.

Curtis looked down and smiled.

"Wolverine," he said. "Excellent choice, Miles." He added *Wolverine* to the list.

"Okay," Curtis said, once the commotion had ceased. "I'm a personal fan of the X-MEN, so we're gonna start off with Wolverine, and then move on to some vehicles. Sketchbooks out!"

The kids dutifully retrieved their sketchbooks from their bags. The quiet one, Miles, pulled out several different pens, lining them up precisely, one by one on the table. Ms. Abraham offered me a seat at the far edge of the table, presumably not to disturb the kids' routine too much. Curtis pulled a spare sketchbook and pen out of his bag and tossed them to me.

"You get to participate, too, Cummings," he said with a wink.

I couldn't help but smile and hold back a couple tears perking at the corners of my eyes. It was clear that these kids were all on the spectrum. And I was absolutely blown away by the care and consideration that Curtis showed them. Not only that, throughout the club, it was clear how much Curtis loved teaching these kids, and how much they liked him, too. He made sure to spend time with each kid, showing them different techniques and genuinely praising each one. At the end of the class, each one came to the front of the room to show their work, and the others all said something they liked about his drawing.

"I like your use of shading."

"I like the action sequence."

Miles would flash his iPad and let Curtis read it aloud each time it was his turn to pay a compliment: "Even though Marvel is *obviously* better—I like the detail on your Batmobile."

"Bethany," Curtis said after the last kid presented. "Would you like to share yours?"

I blushed. "Nah, not this time—I still need a lot of practice," I said. "But I promise I will next time I come—if you'll have me."

Curtis just smiled.

A couple of minutes later, moms were coming in to pick up their kids and admire their handiwork. Curtis sidled up over to me and lowered his voice.

"So, what'd you think?" he asked.

"I'm speechless," I said. "This is amazing. You do this every week?"

"Yeah," he said a little embarrassed, but proud.

"Can I ask, how'd you get into it?"

He paused for a second before answering.

"My older brother, Drew, has Asperger's," he said. "He never had a lot of social things he could do when he was younger and didn't know any other kids like him. School kinda sucked for him. I thought that wasn't really fair, and when I got older, I wanted to see if I could start something. So other kids didn't have to go through that, you know?"

"Sort of, 'when you see a problem, you're anointed to solve it,'" I said, remembering Ash's words.

"Exactly," he said, nodding. "So I got in touch with people from Easter Seals, where Drew used to go for OT, to see if they'd help. And then the library agreed to give us space for free. We've been doing it for about two years."

"That's seriously incredible," I said earnestly. "These kids totally love you, too."

"They're the highlight of my week," he said. "And really, kids with ASD are the best. They're so straightforward, and no one has an ounce of BS in them."

"We could probably all learn a thing or two from them," I agreed. "Though, you're so quiet about this! I had no idea this is how you spent your free time."

He shrugged. "I'd tell anyone who asked," he said. "But if a tree falls in the forest and no one's there to hear it, it still makes a sound, you know."

True.

Then, out of the corner of my eye, I saw someone familiar wander into the room. His whole face broke into a grin when he saw Miles.

"Hey, bud!" he said cheerfully. "Let's see what you've got for me!"

Miles smiled at seeing him as well and showed him his sketchbook.

"Wolverine! He looks awesome. Nice work," he said, giving his shoulder a squeeze.

It was the most genuinely happy I'd ever seen Clay.

He looked up and noticed me noticing him. I gave a small wave in greeting, and he returned it with a slight scowl.

"Let's get going, huh?" he said, quickly ushering Miles toward the door.

"See ya next week, Miles," Curtis said. Miles smiled shyly back. "Bye, Clay," Curtis added.

Clay waved at him with car keys in hand.

I raised an eyebrow at Curtis after he left.

"Clay," I stated, without elaborating. "How…?"

"Miles is his little brother," he said. "He picks him up every week. He *loves* that kid. Though everyone who gets to know him does, too. He may be nonverbal, but he's got a wicked sense of humor," he added.

After closing up shop, we shuffled back to Curtis' car. So many thoughts were going through my head, I couldn't even keep them straight. *Had Curtis known that Clay and I'd had a thing? Did he know Clay was who I wrote about in my column? What if Clay hadn't been ghosting me? What if he'd been going through family stuff he didn't want to tell me about? Or what if he'd ghosted me, but I'd written him off as a horrible person entirely for that one single reason? Geez, I'd purposely hurt Curtis' friend. Are they friends? Things really aren't always black and white, are they?*

Before I knew it, Curtis pulled up in front of my house.

"Thanks for the ride," I said. "And dinner. And, well, for everything. It's been a very…illuminating night," I added.

"Yeah?" he said. "In a good way?"

In a hard way, really. Because shining a light on yourself is the hardest thing to do.

"I hope so," I answered truthfully.

As I closed the car door shut and waved, watching him drive away, two things had never been so clear to me before in my whole life: I had a lot of work to do on myself. And, I knew beyond a doubt that I was falling in love—for real this time.

CHAPTER 26

I didn't fall asleep for hours that night. In the span of that one evening with Curtis, I realized, with my entire body heaving with shame, that I needed to reevaluate basically my entire life, and who—*what*—I had become.

But that really wasn't the worst of it, was it?

The worst—which was becoming clearer to me by the second—was the point system. That was just a hideous thing to do. And stupid! And mean! All the things I detested about my brother. I can't believe I even considered rating Curtis on it.

But the fact that I'd convinced myself that I was going to take Snow Ridge guys down in the name of feminism, that wasn't anything to be proud of either. Maybe I'd helped girls find their voices, but I was kidding myself if I thought that was *really* what my main goal had been all along.

I'd been using other people to my own advantage. I'd been manipulative toward guys to get the reactions I wanted out of them. I'd manipulated my new friends like Lana into following my example. And really, I'd gotten on the paper and written editorials to sway people's opinions not about equal rights, but about *me*.

I'd thought that guys in Snow Ridge were full of themselves. I'd thought they felt like they were entitled. I'd thought they were self-absorbed.

As it turned out, I was the most self-absorbed person in the entire school. And that was never so obvious to me as it was when I spent just a few hours with Curtis. Someone who went so far out of his way to be self*less*. He lifted everyone up—whether it was the kids in his drawing class, or the staff at *The Word,* he found joy in helping other people become the best version of themselves. He saw the good in everyone, and it showed.

I was wracked with shame at how opposite, how far from that mindset I'd been. Geez, no wonder Ash was drifting from me. She had seen the light about all of this earlier, and all I could do was accuse her of ditching me and leaving me hanging. Again, me, me, me.

Well. They say the first step to recovery is recognizing that you have a problem. And by dawn, I'd started to think that maybe, just maybe I could come out on the other side. Because as low as I felt, as ashamed of myself as I was—I thought there was a chance that it wasn't too late. I hadn't inflicted any *major* damage on anyone. I could still give myself an internal makeover. (And, if as a side effect, I'd become the kind of girl who could be with someone as good-hearted as Curtis—well, that would be a fortunate side effect, yes?)

I saw a problem, and I was anointed to solve it. And the fact that *I* was said problem wouldn't deter me.

I was back in *The Word* office after school that following Monday, putting the finishing touches on my editorial. By half past five, it was just Curtis and me in the office. Ever since that night the week before, something had changed between us, that much was clear. Somehow, though, it was different from any other relationship (and I use that term loosely, so take it with a pillar of salt) that I'd had before. When he smiled at me, I felt a hint of butterflies, true, but it was more that I felt warm all over, like the first sip of hot chocolate on a snowy day. When we shared an inside joke, it was like it was our own personal language. Sometimes all he had to do was look at me from across the room and I knew what he was thinking or about to say.

Was this what love felt like? I didn't know from prior experience, but it felt like I'd think it would. And instead of obsessing over Curtis, and wondering what he thought about me, or trying to anticipate, and then manipulate, his next move—I just enjoyed it. Because I knew we would be together. Maybe not today, maybe not tomorrow, but we would be. Someday, and with any luck, someday soon.

I re-read my editorial for the last time, took a deep breath, and e-mailed Curtis my article. I heard it *ding!* on his computer from across the room. I snapped my laptop shut.

"Hey," I called out. "That was me."

"Can't wait to read it," he said mischievously.

"I'd kinda prefer you did wait," I said apologetically. "At least until I'm not in the room."

"No problem."

I started to pack up my bag, slowly and deliberately.

He furrowed his eyebrows.

"You leaving?" he asked.

I shrugged innocently.

"Well, I know you've got your club tonight, and I don't want to impose…" I said.

"That's not imposing," he said firmly. "I was hoping you'd come back. We're still doing superheroes for the next two weeks. And. Ahem. If I remember right, you *promised* you'd share your work this week."

I chuckled. "You win," I said. "Hungry?"

"Always. How about Chinese?" he said, reaching for his jacket.

"Perfect. Can I treat? Feminism means equality, you know."

"I won't argue with that."

Dinner went just as well as the last week's had, if not better—never even a second of awkwardness. We talked a lot about Curtis' plans for University of Michigan next year, and I learned that he was going for their kinesiology program—not the business school, as I'd automatically assumed.

"Ranked number two in the country," he humblebragged.

"Look at you," I said wryly. "Why kinesiology of all things, though?"

"I want to be an occupational therapist," he explained. "I'll have to get my masters, maybe my doctorate one day, but this is the first step. In the long run, I want to work with kids with autism."

Could this guy get any better? Already, Curtis was someone I totally admired, and plus he felt as comfortable as yoga pants. And he made me feel like I comforted him right back. In some ways, he was like a guy version of Ash—except, I wanted to do a few things with (to?) *him* that I'd never wanted to do with my best female friend.

We headed to the library for the club, and already, I could tell my presence didn't throw the kids off like it had the week before. I was glad that I'd been accepted as a safe piece of the scenery.

"'Kay, guys," Curtis started off, once everyone was in their seats. "This week we're designing our own superheroes. Let's make them have their own unique backstories and powers. I want to see your own creativity shine through—course, I'm happy to help wherever you need it."

I bit my lip to hide my smile. I knew exactly what I'd be drawing that night.

Curtis wandered the room throughout the class, stopping at each kid's spot to help him out and discuss the characters. When he made his way over to me, though, I flipped my sketchbook over and smirked.

"No peeking," I said.

"All right, all right," he said, holding up his hands.

At the end of class, each kid took his turn to show his superhero. Then I went up to share mine.

"I didn't follow the rules, and I made two. I'm calling this first one Justice," I said. I'd drawn a dark-haired girl with legal scales on the front of her flattering, yet tasteful, bodysuit. "She eliminates double standards in a single bound. Closes the pay gap with her magic wand. Rewrote history books just by entering the library. Her biggest achievement is giving voices back to those who lost them in the Valley of Silence."

The kids looked sort of confused, but Curtis chuckled. I took a deep breath and flipped my notepad to the next page.

"And her counterpart—her equal counterpart—is Captain Kindness," I said, displaying my drawing to the class. I'd gone with the loopy, rounded, Archie-cartoon style rather than the harsh, jagged lines found in darker comics, and drawn a peace symbol on the front of his unitard. "He can broker peace deals in the blink of an eye. End wars with the snap of his fingers. Holds the door open and always brakes for squirrels."

Curtis was definitely blushing by now. The superhero *did* have his brown curls.

I continued, "What's great about Captain Kindness is that he only uses his powers for good, and never evil. He doesn't have a single mean bone in his body, and even better, when people are around him, they feed off his kindness like vampires hungry for happiness. So the next thing you know, you've got a whole army of kindness champions out there, trying to make the world a better place. He's an inspiration. To me, anyway."

By then, I was looking right at Curtis and those soft brown eyes of his.

"Why are you all red, Curtis?" asked one of the boys.

He coughed. "No reason. Anyway, great job everyone, and we'll see you next week!"

Well, I'd done it. I'd made myself as clear as I comfortably could. And if Curtis didn't pick up what I was putting down, there was little else I could do. And if that was the case, so be it.

We were both a little nervous on the ride home—I was, anyway, and Curtis was quieter than usual. A few minutes later, he pulled me into my driveway, and there we were.

"So," I said. "Thanks. Again. Really."

"No problem," he said, looking me in the forehead.

Awkward pause.

"Um. I guess I should go inside."

He looked like he was about to say something but didn't.

Did I just totally blow it? I did. I blew it.

"So. See you tomorrow?" I asked hesitantly, unbuckling my seatbelt.

"Yeah, sounds good," he said. Maybe he was relieved that I was finally getting out of his car.

"Okay. Bye."

I went inside. My parents weren't home—they'd taken some of my dad's clients to a Cubs game. I pulled a mug from the cabinet, made myself some tea, and sat at the kitchen table, with my laptop in front of me. In the past week, I'd come up with a new grand master plan—one that I was creating for reasons far more right than wrong—and one that would be a lot less self-serving in the long-run. I was about to send off some e-mails when I heard a knock at the front door.

Confused, I opened it to find Curtis standing in front of me.

"Hey, what's up?" I asked, cocking my head. "Everything okay?"

"Yeah, no," he said, fidgeting a little. "I just forgot to do something."

"What?"
"To ask if I could kiss you."
I smiled. "I'd been hoping you would already."
And he leaned in.

CHAPTER 27

A week later, my piece ran in *The Word.* It was the proudest I'd ever been to have my name attached to the term "Tell Me What You Really Think."

A New Tree

Have you ever felt like you'd been going the wrong direction in your life? I have. And when it became obvious to me, I wanted not only to turn over a new leaf—I wanted to rip out the whole tree by the roots and plant a new one altogether.

I've realized that I've gotten a lot of living in Snow Ridge for nearly 17 years—but, I haven't given a lot. And that's something I want to change, so today, I'm turning over a new leaf. Are you in?

Let's make things better, kinder and easier for people. I've got a couple of ideas to start:

- **Leggings for the Library**. Our administration has agreed that next Monday, anyone—male or female, mind you—can come to school in leggings for a $5 donation, which will be collected by your first-period teacher. All proceeds will be donated to the special needs youth programs at the Snow Ridge Public Library.
- **Just One Lunch.** For legal reasons, the school's not backing this, but I have permission to lead it on my own. Skip lunch on Wednesday next week to get an appreciation of what real hunger is like, and donate the $5 you'd have spent to the Countywide Food Bank. Curtis Snyder will collect cash in B lunch and I'll collect for C lunch. (Any volunteers for A lunch? Let me know!)

- **Cans and Clothes.** We'll have bins in the Commons all week long. Bring in canned food and gently used clothes and deposit them in the orange bins. On Friday, I'll bring the donations to Butterflies, a local shelter for survivors of domestic violence.

  Want to help out, but in your own way instead? Visit volunteermatch.org and find your own cause to fight for.

  Thanks for joining me.

And, the feedback from that article was overwhelming—more than I ever could have expected. I got a standing ovation in Media Studies (even from a begrudging Lindsay) that day, and I didn't go to a class all week without positive comments about it from classmates, guys and girls alike. But, and I mean this sincerely, that's not why I did it. I meant every word I said in that article, and I wanted to reframe my mindset. Worrying about leggings and the dress code? I'd turn it into something the school could get behind and have an event to benefit Curtis' cartoonists. Upset about lunch table politics? Let's think about people who have actual problems at lunchtime—like not having enough to eat. Wasting anger on being ghosted by a guy like Clay? I'd rather channel it into helping women who *really* had suffered from bad treatment by men.

I may have gotten girls at this school charged up and ready to self-advocate, but that wasn't enough. Because life wasn't about an "us versus them" mindset, whether we were talking female and male, red versus blue, you versus me. We needed to work together and look out for one another. We all belonged to each other.

The only person who wasn't thrilled by my article? Of all people, Harrison.

When I'd landed in my chair in Spanish at the end of the day, he'd given me a withering look.

"What's with you?" I asked bluntly, raising an eyebrow. Since falling for Curtis, I'd found myself treating Harrison like just a friend rather than a crush and thinking about him hardly at all.

"Nothing," he said innocently. "I read *The Word* today, and I was just wondering what happened to the Bethany I knew and loved. Who replaced her with such a little do-gooder? C'mon."

I was completely taken aback, and before I knew it, too many thoughts were horseracing through my head.

Knew and loved*? You've had a weird way of showing it, pal.*

Why would he say that if he didn't mean it?

What's so bad about wanting to do good things?

Loved?

Wait. Curtis, Curtis, Curtis.

"Vamonos, clase," Sr. Applebaum had droned, before I'd even had a chance to reply, and so I didn't. But I stewed on it all through class. I was never so happy to rush out of class when the bell rang and head back upstairs to *The Word* office, Curtis, and all the warm fuzzies they both inherently brought me.

While I think Curtis liked the new me just fine, I think he liked the revitalized energy that the *new*-new me had. Also, I can't say I didn't love the extra glances he'd sneak at me during class or in *The Word* office after school. And the rides home he gave me each day. And the kisses at the end of each ride.

Ash had been hard to pin down, between this CJ guy and working at her photography gigs down in the southwest suburbs—she was even going up there after school most days—but she'd jumped at the chance to help me with this latest plan. We came in early to put up posters and flyers the week before the events. She also took pictures of people posing hard in their leggings all day—guys and girls, teachers and students—and posted them with #leggingsforthelibrary. Everyone got a huge kick out of it! Overall, people chipped in a whopping $5,050 for the library.

Just One Lunch ended up being a hit, too. Ash and I had brought horseshoes, a few Frisbees, and her dad's game of bags to set up in the quad during lunch to help keep people's minds off their growling stomachs, which seemed to work. Jono Trubisky, Snow Ridge's mascot, (aka Reinhard the Rhino) hosted a lip sync battle during his lunch period, which I wish I could have seen but heard it was epic. And then, I was shocked that Clay of all people had volunteered to collect the cash for A lunch. It felt like we'd reached a détente. Between the three lunch periods, we'd collected nearly a thousand dollars for the food bank.

And, Cans and Clothes turned out to be a massive, massive success. So much so that we had to get extra bins Wednesday, and Ash had to take her mom's minivan to school that Friday so that we could bring everything to the shelter in one haul. After the janitors helped us lug the dollies with the bins to the loading dock and loaded up the minivan, Ash and I headed toward the shelter.

Once we'd arrived, the shelter's outreach coordinator came out to greet us, and several of the women staying there poked their heads out to see everything we were lugging in. On our second trip, three of them came out to join us, holding the door open and helping us maneuver the boxes into the kitchen, as wide-eyed toddlers darted in and out of the room. One woman held the door open for us the whole time, broadly smiling—she looked about eight months pregnant, and maybe a year or two older than me. Everyone we met gave us a huge hug on our way out.

Next, we stopped at the food bank to drop off the money we'd collected at lunch on Wednesday. Their development director hugged us, took a picture with us and gave us a tour. There was a volunteer group in the warehouse finishing up their last load of weekend backpacks, full of food—they distributed these on Fridays to the hundreds of local kids that relied on school lunches, so that they'd have something to eat over the weekend. I'd had no idea that this kind of poverty, so close to Snow Ridge, even existed.

Our next stop was at the Snow Ridge Public Library, to present them with the $5,050 check. The head librarian opened the envelope, looked at the check and started crying.

By the time we got back in the car, we felt exhausted but exhilarated.

"Seriously, Ash, thanks so much for helping me out with this all week," I said, fanning my neck with my ponytail.

"Of course, babe," she said, checking her blindspot before turning out of the parking lot. "Happy to do it. And besides, I haven't gotten to see enough of you lately."

"So true," I agreed.

"And I know a lot of that's my fault," Ash admitted. "I've been doing my own thing more often than not. But—that's changing soon."

"Why?"

"Well, college semester ends next week."

I'd nearly forgotten—May was right around the corner.

"Oh," I said realizing what she meant. "Is CJ going home for the summer? Do you think your parents would let you go visit him?"

"I'm sure of it," she said. "He's actually from Snow Ridge."

"You're kidding!" I said incredulously. "Where does he live? Do I know him?" My mind raced as I tried to think of any older guys from town named CJ.

Ash took a deep breath.

"That's the thing," she said. "All right. Don't hate me."

And then. I knew it before she even said it.

"No," I said under my breath, my face darkening.

She looked at me meekly.

"CJ is *Christian*?" I sputtered. "How in the hell could you not tell me this?"

"Because I knew you'd freak out!" Ash said defensively.

"Of course I'm freaking out! He's my brother," I shrieked. "And you totally lied to me."

"I didn't *totally* lie."

"Oh, *please*. You both did. Him, I expect that. But *you*?"

"It happened the way I told you! He *did* come up to me in the Chipotle. I'd barely remembered meeting him in front of your house that day."

"Wow," I muttered. "So does he actually go by 'CJ' now or was that just something you guys made up to trick me?"

"He does—that's what everyone at Habitat in Australia called him, and it stuck. And everything else I've told you about us is completely true, for that matter," Ash insisted. "Being down there changed him. He told me that he never realized how good he had it before, and that now that he's been around people who'd been homeless, it totally changed his perspective.

Did you know he's thinking about switching his major to nonprofit management?"

"Oh, I'm sure that'll last," I snapped. "Saint Christian, all the way."

"Bethany! He's a really sweet guy."

"The sweetest. Ever."

Ignoring me, Ash continued, "The thing is, not only do I like him, but he appreciates me right back. He cares what I think and encourages me. When I'm around him, it feels like…like home. And isn't that what matters?"

Isn't the fact that you're my best friend what matters?

I didn't answer her. Instead, I asked, "Do my parents know about you two yet?"

She pursed her lips.

"Not exactly," she admitted. "We were gonna wait until he's back in town for the summer before we told them."

"Ah."

"What, 'ah?'"

"You're expecting that he's going to introduce you as his actual girlfriend to people."

Ash scowled. "What the hell's that supposed to mean?"

"I don't think you should get your hopes up, because he's going to just get sick of you and toss you aside," I said. "And did you ever realize that he's probably had *you* on the point system this whole time?"

She turned beet red as she pulled into my driveway

I opened the door and said to her, seething, "Don't come crawling to me when he dumps your ass because I don't think I can hold back an 'I told you so.'"

Then I slammed the door behind me as hard as I could.

CHAPTER 28

Ash peeled off, and pissed as she was, I knew she wasn't dumb enough to text and drive. So, before I even went inside my house, I dialed up Christian on Facetime.

He answered, looking like he'd just been woken up from a nap.

"Sup?" he asked, rubbing his eyes.

"What the hell is wrong with you?!" I screamed at him. "You absolute piece of—"

"Oh, so Ash told you," he said with a yawn.

"You know what, Christian?" I hissed. "You may have fooled her into thinking you're a great guy now. You may have fooled this town your whole life. You may have fooled Mom and Dad. But you will *never, ever fool me*."

"Hey, now—"

"And 'Nonprofit Management?' Is that even a thing?"

"Of course it's a thing," he said, annoyed. "There's a huge need for it. Nonprofits are–"

"Please. Like Dad's *not* gonna just hand you the keys to his office one day," I huffed. "Anyway, that's totally beside the point. The point is that you have no right stealing my best friend away from me."

"Well, you can't steal something that wants to be stolen, can you?" he said, eyes narrowing at me. "She's with me out of her own free will. It's not like I put a gun to her head."

"Christian—excuse me, I mean *CJ*," I said, rolling my eyes. "There are legit thousands of girls at your school. And you can't be with one of them instead?"

"There's no one like Ash," he said with a grin, ruffling his hair in a way that she probably loved. Ugh.

I smirked. "Oh, I don't know," I said smoothly. "I'm sure she's like some other girls you know. Like Kelsey Stevenson. Or like Jess McNair. You know, girls who like to really, let's say, *keep it one hundred*."

All the color drained from his ultra-tanned face.

"What," he said quietly.

"That's right, dumbass," I sneered. "Next time you give me your secondhand electronics, make sure you empty the digital trash first."

He looked physically sick.

"Did you tell Ash?" he finally asked.

"Oh, she knows," I confirmed, adding out of fairness, "Believe it or not, she knew before she even met you. And for some reason unclear to me, she likes you anyway."

"Oh," he said, hugely relieved.

"In fact," I added, "We've been using your system to rate guys all freaking year. So have half the girls in Snow Ridge. So she's probably been keeping score on *you* all along." Okay, that was unlikely, but I had to scare him a little.

It seemed to work. He looked awestruck. And ashamed.

But that wasn't enough.

"So here's the deal, Christian," I said. "You're gonna back off Ash. Or I'm showing your point system to Mom and Dad. And you can see what your summer looks like after that. No, see what your *entire life* looks like after that."

His face darkened. "You think you can blackmail me?"

"No," I said innocently. "I think I can persuade you to do the right thing, for once in your life."

And before he could even answer, I hung up on him.

CHAPTER 29

The weekend was pretty much crap after that. I was still seething over Ash and Christian and could think of little else but their betrayal. The next week started off a little better though: on Monday, Curtis asked me to prom.

Without any ridiculous fanfare, or for the sake of making a viral video, or spectacle that was more for everyone else to enjoy. No, he just nonchalantly brought it up when driving me home after *The Word*.

"I actually wasn't even gonna go to prom," he confessed. "But that was before I had anyone I wanted to go with."

"Oh, so you do now?" I teased. "Who's the lucky girl?"

He was taken aback for a second before he realized I was just kidding.

"What, do I gotta get down on one knee to ask?" he said mischievously. "Should I pull over?"

"No," I said, giggling. "Though it can't hurt to ask me properly."

At that, he did pull over, threw the gear into park, and tapped on his hazards. He then faced me and took my hands in his.

"Bethany Cummings," he said without a hint of irony. "Will you go to prom with me?"

My heart melted just a little bit. Okay, a lot.

"Absolutely," I whispered, before leaning in for a kiss.

I floated on air the rest of the afternoon.

Then, around 11 that night, I was finishing up my English Lit essay when I got an email notification in the corner of the screen. I checked it, and it was an invite from Lana to a shared Google Doc. Titled "Snow Ridge Point System."

Oh, no.

I wish I could tell you it's what I thought it was, but that would be an understatement.

It was as if the point system that Ash and I had used earlier was a marshmallow, and now it had been put in a microwave.

There were literally hundreds of pages—one for nearly every guy in the school with scores from multiple girls. It was freaking color coded.

This had been a *way* bigger deal than I thought. And it wasn't just public, as in "a few girls from FEC and their friends know" public. No, this was *public*. Paper trail public.

I frantically searched for Clay's page first, to see if there was anything self-incriminating there. Nothing. Whew.

And, holy crap. There was a page for Curtis. Lots of colors to represent different girls on there—all for acts of chivalry. No surprise there, really. And then 20 points in a bright pink, for asking to prom.

Dammit. I had texted Lana to tell her earlier today. She must have put that in there and made my color pussyhat pink.

But then I continued to scroll all the way through the spreadsheet and noticed that there was an appendix at the end.

And the very first entry in it said:

"The female population of Snow Ridge is grateful to Bethany Cummings and Ash Bauer for their insight and gift in developing the point system for Snow Ridge High School."

I immediately deleted the sentence, saved the document, and then slammed my computer shut. But I knew the damage had been done.

The next morning, I cornered Lana as soon as I saw her pull into the parking lot.

"Hey," I said, hopping in her car before she even turned it off. "So that spreadsheet you sent me. What's the deal?"

"What do you mean?" she asked brightly.

"Like, why does it exist, and how many people know about this?"

She chuckled. "Well, I was talking with the girls after my party, and we realized it would be way more efficient if it was a shared doc—that way, we could see what everyone else said. You know, kind of like Rate My Teacher!"

"So who's seen it?"

"I don't know. There's probably like.... I don't know, all the FECers on it. I just finished compiling it and sent it around to everyone—plus you and Ash—late last night. Well, and I sent it to Kaia. I thought it would set a good example for her. She's had her share of guys treat her badly already."

I blanched.

"You sent it to your little sister—the cheerleader?" I said aghast. "Do you think there's a chance she might have said something about it, or forwarded it to someone else? Or screen-shotted it? You know how fast word spreads around here."

"I don't think she would do that," she said, shaking her head but seeming a little less sure of herself.

"Not only is there a chance this is gonna get around—who put me and Ash in the appendix?"

Lana was quiet for a second, then said, "Well, I wanted to give credit where credit was due. Like, to honor you two."

"Oh my God," I murmured.

The minute bell rang, and I made my way to class, feeling sick to my stomach. I got there just as the bell sounded and slid into my seat next to Ash (who made no recognition of my presence). And nearly every set of eyes in the room were on us.

Except for Curtis. He was sitting far across the room from me and staring intently at the table instead.

No. Please, God, no.

Just then, Ms. Knox came in with a box containing a cheese Danish and tossed it on the table.

"Morning, guys," she said brightly. "I think we've got Lauren and Wes presenting today, yes?"

And then class began, with me feeling more unnerved by the second, with nothing I could do about it.

Curtis wouldn't meet my eyes once throughout class.

As soon as the bell rang, I scrambled out of my seat and over to him.

"What's going on?" I murmured breathlessly, reaching my hand out to his.

He pulled his hand sharply back, like he'd been stung. He then met my eyes and glowered.

"You know, I thought I actually meant something to you," he said, his voice brimming with ice water. "And I guess I do mean something. I just thought I was more than a point value to you."

Feign innocence. Feign innocence.

"What?" I said, my face burning and heart pounding. "What are you talking about?"

His eyes filled with so much hurt I almost instinctively reached out for him again but stopped myself.

"Don't treat me like I'm stupid," he said in a near growl. "Just do yourself a favor and reset my score to zero." With that, he threw his messenger bag over one shoulder and stormed out of the office.

I froze in place, then felt a tap on my shoulder.

I whirled around to find Ash, who'd been hovering a few steps behind me.

"Dude," she said, her eyes wide. "What is happening?"

I took a deep breath and held onto her arm as we shuffled out the door. We hadn't made up yet—far from it—but I couldn't *not* talk to her about this.

"I think Curtis found out about the point system," I said in a small voice, tears pricking at my eyes. "And I'm almost positive other people know about it, too. Okay, not just other people. *Everyone*."

Ash looked like she'd just been punched.

"No," she whispered. "How?"

"Have you checked your email?" I asked. "Did you see one from Lana?"

"Not yet. Why? What did she say?"

After I explained what had happened, Ash could hardly look me in the eyes, either.

"I'm really sorry," I said weakly.

Ash blew out her bangs.

"I just wish you would have deleted the whole thing before you ever told anyone," she said, picking at a fingernail. "I mean, *I* did. Forever ago. Like, right after me and Trevor ended."

"I know."

"And I told you it was a terrible idea. Multiple times."

"I know."

"This sucks," she said. A moment later, she added, "But I know it's gonna suck worse for you. Because I don't know how Curtis could get over this."

"I know," I said glumly, realizing just how right she was. I mean really, what could I say?

Though I couldn't help but add, "At least you don't have to worry about Christian caring, amirite?"

"Actually, you're not right at all," Ash said, glaring. "Because he dumped me on Saturday."

"He did?" I said in disbelief.

"Yeah. Said things were 'getting too serious' and it was over. I would have told my best friend, but I didn't want to *come crawling back and hear I told you so*."

With that, she stomped off—but then she turned around to ream me out some more.

"You know what else? You know why Shane, and all those other guys totally backed off of you after your freshman Homecoming? It's because *Christian* had heard about what a creep he'd been to you, and threatened to kick the ass of any guy who disrespected his sister. Who even *looked* at you the wrong way."

My eyes bugged out of my head.

"What?"

"Oh, yeah. In fact, he threw Shane up against the wall in the boys' locker room and gave him a minor concussion. He knew what a bunch of assholes those guys were, and he spent your first two years of high school trying to protect you. Without ever saying a thing. So don't act like he's the world's biggest jerk. He might not be perfect, but no one is. Not even you."

CHAPTER 30

If there was any day that skipping school was the right answer, it was today. I walked the two miles home and told my mom I felt sick to my stomach (not a lie), and she called me out of school. The rest of the day I spent at home alternating between naps, feeling like the human equivalent of a stale rice cake, and starting off dozens of texts to Christian, Ash, and Curtis before ultimately deleting every one of them. I didn't know what I could possibly say to them, let alone the entire Snow Ridge High School student body.

It was true that I'd done some things to be proud of to this school. But it felt like they were instantly negated by the exposure of the point system. It showed exactly who I was: a loser, a joke. A fraud. I'd had no problem sharing my feelings in *The Word*, when they could be painted over with a thick layer of snark, but now?

As the day went on, I was thinking more in terms of damage control. I could even just pretend it was a total joke. Just laugh it off. Like, "What kind of idiot would even *believe* that I was serious?" Ash would be on board with that. And with any luck, Curtis would believe it, too. I'd swear up and down to him that it was all a stupid joke, if that meant I could get things back to the way they were between us.

Right?

I still hadn't figured out what my next move would be when I had to return to school the next day. Media Studies was just as ice-cold as it had been the day before, if not worse—even Ms. Knox was looking at me sideways.

She'd heard, too.

But it wasn't a relief when I was summoned out of class because of where I had to go next.

I slowly turned the doorknob to Dean Squared's office. He was already at his desk, waiting for me, his fingertips touching each other.

"Miss Cummings," he said coolly, nodding toward the seat.

I sat down and cleared my throat.

"Dean Dean."

"Are you quite well, Miss Cummings," he stated rather than asked. "I understand you were ill yesterday."

"Yes," I said, steeling myself. "A 24-hour bug."

"Ah."

I sat silently, waiting for him to continue.

"You do know why you're here, don't you?" he asked.

Here it comes. You can do this, Bethany.

"Have I done something wrong?" I asked, voice steady.

He gave a small mirthful laugh.

"Have you?" he asked. "Have you, indeed?"

"I'm asking you," I said, adding, "Sir."

"I saw that…document that mentioned you," he said, cutting to the chase.

Must have gotten around to Seamus. Crap.

"It's pretty unbelievable, isn't it?" I said, shaking my head. "Who would do such a thing? I mean, I can't think of *anyone* who would want to smear my good name. Or Ash Bauer's. *Anyone* at all." I then glared at the framed photo of Seamus on his desk.

When I had turned my head back toward him, he looked at me levelly.

"The issue here is not someone 'smearing your good name,' as you call it," he said, voice nearing a growl. "The issue is bullying. The same issue that you sat in this very seat over, not three months ago."

"You're going to accept that this—this—*propaganda*—is automatically true?" I asked, raising an eyebrow. "Rather than trying to find the perpetrator? Because listing me specifically in that 'document' seems a lot like bullying to me."

Sorry, Lana. Watch out for that bus.

His lips formed a thin, tight line.

"So," I asked, pulling my backpack onto my lap. "Can I go?"

He looked at me, his mouth puckering like he'd just bitten into something unpleasant. Which I suppose, he had.

He briefly nodded to me in dismissal. My hand was on the knob when he said, "Miss Cummings?"

I paused, then turned back around to face him.

"You reap what you sow," he said, then returned to the paperwork on his desk.

I swiftly left, shut the door behind me, and collected myself. It had taken every nerve I had to not fold like a losing hand of poker under Dean Squared's glare. But, if I had any hope of making it through this week, let alone the rest of my junior year, I had to keep my resolve and come up with a plan.

I couldn't go home sick two days in a row—my mom would definitely know something was up—so I had to make it through the rest of the school day. I kept my head down, refusing to look at anyone in my classes though I felt eyes constantly burning into me like a hot poker. I hid in the library at lunch. And by the time I got to Spanish at the end of the day, I was totally exhausted.

I slid into my seat and started pulling out my notebook when I heard a voice beside me.

"Hey," said Harrison softly.

"Oh, hey," I said, a little puzzled. Didn't he know what a piece of garbage I was?

"You doing okay?" he asked, without any extra explanation.

I bit my lip and willed my eyes to keep from welling up. I just nodded.

"Just wanted to tell you to keep your head up," he said.

"Thanks," I said.

He was about to go back to his desk and then changed his mind. He leaned back down and said, "Also. I heard you and Curtis are kaput."

This startled me. Harrison knew Curtis and I had gotten together in the first place? And for that matter, how'd he hear Curtis and I *were* officially kaput—when even I wasn't 100 percent sure? Sheesh, what else did Harrison know?

"Did you?" I eventually said.

"Yeah," he said, leaning forward and twirling the pen between his fingers. "You wanna talk about it…maybe later tonight?"

Did I want to? My brain said no, but my body said yes. My heart started to pound, and I found my hands starting to tingle. I knew my parents were going to be gone most of the evening, moving Christian out of school for the summer. They wouldn't be back 'til late.

"Um, yeah," I said. "How about you come by around seven?"

"Cool," he said, putting the pen back in his mouth. "I'll see you then."

CHAPTER 31

That afternoon, I tried to concentrate on my homework, but I just couldn't. Too many thoughts were going through my head.

The doorbell rang exactly at seven.

"Hey, Harrison," I said, motioning him inside.

"Hey," he said, with his trademark cocky grin.

He looked like he'd just come from lacrosse club—hair still glistening with sweat, grass stains on his Under Armour shirt and low-slung shorts. And, when he leaned in to hug me, I noticed a whiff of Altoids.

"Can I get you something to drink?"

"That'd be great."

We got some drinks from the fridge, ambled into the den, and flopped onto the sectional. I switched on the TV for background noise—HGTV was still on from the day before. We made small talk for a little while before he got serious.

"So. You doing okay?" he asked, nudging my foot with his. A small electric current ran through me.

"Not really," I said. "I'm a little stressed about it. After that whole—thing this week."

"Ah, don't worry about it," he said, waving it off. "Everyone knows that point system is a bunch of crap."

"You think so? I mean, don't just tell me what you think I want to hear. Be honest. Does everyone blame me and Ash for it?"

"I think people are smart enough to think for themselves, and not let other people's opinions bother them," he said diplomatically. "I'm sure you realize this, but Curtis, by default? Not that smart."

Curtis. Hearing the name come out of Harrison's mouth just felt wrong. As was Harrison's assessment of him.

"*But*," he added.

I raised an eyebrow.

"It did get me thinking," he continued. "What if you really *were* the mastermind behind it?"

"Oh?" I asked, feeling my pulse quicken.

"Yeah. I mean, taking no prisoners. Getting what you want. Teaching Snow Ridge girls to kick ass and take names, literally. Then as soon as you had them in the palm of your hand, rip their hearts out."

"Oh?" I repeated.

His eyes had a bit of a wicked gleam in them.

"Yeah. That seemed…kinda badass. Like a Bond girl. Kinda hot." He edged a little closer to me on the couch.

"Oh," I said, a little breathlessly.

"Yeah," he said, looking me in the eyes, the way I'd always wanted him to. The way I'd always dreamed he would, if he could only see what was right in front of him. If he could only see the real me.

And you know how I felt, looking right back at him?

Hollow.

Evidently, the version of me that I'd created months ago? The me that kicked people when they were down? The me that went out of her way to be hurtful? *That* was the me he wanted. He'd admitted to me a long time ago that he was a glutton for punishment. Even if that was the case, I couldn't be the one to dole it out. Not anymore.

Harrison closed his eyes and started to lean forward.

"Um," I said, abruptly standing up. "You know, it's getting kinda late. And I still have a column to write for *The Word* by tomorrow." I folded my arms across my chest and started tapping my foot.

He opened his eyes wide.

"Oh," he said, clearing his throat. "Should I get going?"

"Probably," I said, and made for the front door. I held it wide open for him, ushering him to it.

Still looking bewildered, Harrison gave me a side-hug and walked through the door.

"Bethany?" he said.

I raised my eyebrows back at him.

"Did I do something wrong?" he asked, looking at me with sad, puppydog eyes.

It almost physically hurt me to say it, but I had to be straight with him.

"No, you didn't," I said. "*I* did. But I can't anymore. Goodnight," I added, and firmly shut the door before racing back upstairs. I had work to do.

CHAPTER 32

I went to my room and furiously started to type. I had something to say, and this time, I wasn't going to leave anything ambiguous.

But an hour later, I heard the garage door open. My heart started thumping, knowing that my parents were home with Christian.

I crept downstairs.

"Hey," I said, gesturing toward the boxes. "You guys need a hand?"

"Maybe tomorrow," Mom said, fanning herself with her shirt. "I think we'll wait 'til then to unload everything. Tonight was enough work."

"I'm going to pick up some sandwiches," Dad said. "We didn't even stop for dinner."

"Ooh, I'll come with," Mom said. "Christian, you want anything?"

He looked at me coldly. "No thanks, Mom."

"Bethany?" she asked.

"I'm good, thanks."

"We'll be back in 20," Dad said, and the two of them hopped back in the car.

Christian started to wordlessly trudge up the stairs.

"Hey," I said. "Can we talk?"

He turned around.

"About what? Anything else you wanted to lord over my head?"

"That's fair," I said. "Look. I wanted to say I'm sorry."

He cocked his head to the side, came back down the stairs, leaned against the banister and folded his arms.

"Really."

"I didn't understand how much you and Ash really cared about each other," I admitted. "And I realize how much it sucks to have that kind of thing taken away from you. Whether it was fairly or, you know, unfairly."

He softened, just slightly.

"And you know this how?"

"Well. Let's just say he *wasn't* one of the guys whose ass you threatened to kick two years ago."

He chuckled. "So Ash told you about that, too."

"She only just told me. I'd had no idea," I said, adding, "Not that I really condone you getting all in my business and eliminating my social life for two years. That sucked. But I do see that your heart was in the right place, kind of."

"You are my sister, you know."

"I know."

We were quiet.

"So. Who's the guy whose ass I need to kick now?"

"You don't need to kick anyone's ass, but it's Curtis Snyder."

He was clearly taken aback. "Curtis Snyder wouldn't hurt a fly if someone tried to waterboard him into it. He hurt you?"

"No, no. It's me who hurt him."

And I told him all that had happened in the past few days. Having broken up with Ash, he'd had no idea. And when I told him that Ash was listed on the master document that got around as well, he looked like he was on the verge of tears.

"God," he said, shaking his head. "I am so, so unbelievably sorry I ever started that whole stupid point system."

I hesitated, then said, "I have to ask. How'd you get the idea?"

He took a deep breath.

"You're not gonna believe me."

"Try me," I offered.

"Well. When I was in eighth grade, I had a huge crush on…" his voice lowered, and he coughed.

"Who?" I asked, raising an eyebrow.

"Lindsay."

I stifled a laugh.

"Shut up," he said. "It was a long time ago."

"Okay," I said politely.

He squinched his eyes shut. "And we started like, making out after school sometimes. Well, for her, it was probably just making out, but I was like…oh God, this is so embarrassing, but

I thought I was really in love with her. I even wrote her a poem."

Don't laugh, don't laugh, that's mean.

"Then what?" I prodded.

"After I gave her the poem, the very next day, she dumped me, telling me I was too clingy. And after that, I was like, broken. You don't even know how bad it hurt. It was five years ago, and it still sucks to think about it. So right then, I swore I was never gonna let a girl hurt me again. And I thought about it, and we were just learning how to do math in Excel, and I don't know, I just kinda came up with the idea."

"Wow," I said, incredulous. "Did you ever tell anyone? About the spreadsheet, not Lindsay."

"Are you kidding? No way—to either. And after high school, I was like, forget it, this is ridiculous, so I just trashed it."

"Huh."

"I even thought about it when I met Ash actually, but I knew after one single day with her that I'd *never* put her on a point system. Because I wasn't gonna let her go unless I was forced to." He looked pointedly at me.

I reddened.

"Yeah. About that," I said. "Well, you might as well beg Ash's forgiveness, because a, you'll never find a better girlfriend than her, and b, I'm not gonna blackmail you. I swear I won't tell Mom and Dad that *you* had anything to do with it. Though, I am coming clean about my role in the point system."

"Really?"

"I can't live a lie," I said. "I have to own up to what I did wrong if I'm ever gonna move forward in my life. No one made me do this but me, you know. I have to accept responsibility for it. Come what may."

"Wow," he said, scratching at the scruff on his chin. "Mom and Dad are gonna kill you, you know."

"I know," I said, adding wryly. "But it's the right thing to do."

"Godspeed," he said saluting me.

I laughed. "Well, I'm going upstairs," I said. "Gotta finish my column-slash-confession."

I headed back to my room, closed the door behind me and resumed typing.

Another half hour passed by—I heard my parents come back in from grabbing dinner and then shuffle off to bed—and I had my column nearly done. I was just about to print it out when I saw a Facebook notification pop up in the corner of my screen.

That's weird. Who even uses Facebook?

I clicked on it and saw that it was the one thing people use Facebook for these days—a streaming Facebook Live video—and saw that it was coming from Christian. Wearing a huge, cocky smile and a Snow Ridge High t-shirt.

Oh, my God.

"Hey guys, what's up," he said, and I heard the slight echo from those words coming from the other side of my bedroom wall.

"Just here to say I've been catching up on everything Snow Ridge since I made it back to town for the summer, and, ah, I'm a little disappointed. Not in Snow Ridge High—go Rhinos, whoo!—but in myself."

What?

"The thing is, my little sister Bethany—you may know her because she's this whipsmart, hilarious junior and all around badass—well, she was sick of being treated like crap by the guys in her life. Of course she came to yours truly for advice, being her big bro and all. And I came up with this system where she should score and rate guys, so that she could decide when to dump them.

"Now, she thought that was hilarious. Hilariously *mean*, and she was like, 'Christian, why would you suggest that? This is a horrible, awful thing…"

At this point, my column had finished printing. I yanked it off my printer and trotted into Christian's bedroom.

"Oh, hey!" he said, seeing me come in.

"Leave it on," I said, sidling up next to him on his bed, not even caring that I was in my raggedy pajamas and glasses for the night.

"What?"

"Christian," I said impatiently. "You don't have to do this. I have something to say, too." I hoisted up the sheets of paper in front of me.

"You sure."

"Yes," I said emphatically.

"Well," he said, trying to keep looking cool for the camera. "You've always been better with words than me. Floor's yours."

"Thank you," I said, then looked into the camera. "Okay. Here goes."

I began to read.

"I've lived in Snow Ridge my whole life, but it wasn't until a kindred spirit moved to town that I finally felt like I was at home. Because when I met her, I knew I'd met the kindest, most decent, most true friend I'd ever known. And I felt like it was the two of us against the world—but it wasn't. And that's where I made my first mistake.

"It's a funny process to find your way sometimes, isn't it? For me, I think I've used my biting sense of humor as a way in, but as it turned out, it was more of a defense mechanism. And a lot of the time, it's not as hilarious as I'd like to think. It's hurtful. Which made me hurtful by default.

"You see, I'd been feeling like I'd been on the bottom rung in life for so long, that I'd simply had enough of it. And, I convinced Ash Bauer, my best friend, to go along with me on a ridiculous plan to get back at the guys of Snow Ridge, by giving what I considered a dose of their own medicine."

At this point I stopped reading, then looked directly in the camera.

"We used Christian's suggestion—that's true—but Ash wouldn't have known about it if I hadn't told her, and I accept full responsibility for digging this up and keeping it alive."

I then resumed my article. "It was all for the sake of getting people to see me as a 'leader,' and climb my way to the top here. Pretty pathetic of me, right?

"And I'd like to say that, to the people I've hurt—actually, to everyone in this school, whether my actions affected you or not—I am deeply sorry. It was wrong of me. There's no excuse for regarding and treating people the way I did.

"Additionally, I would like to clarify that, out of loyalty to me and wanting to see me succeed, Ash went along with my idea. And please—don't blame her in any way because the idea was mine and mine alone.

"I learned a lot about myself these past few months—the hard way. What I especially learned was how little I wanted to be the person I'd become.

"Along the way, I met someone who opened my eyes to a different way of thinking, and, I believe, helped save me from myself.

"It's because of this person that I realized a lot of things. Namely, that life's painful enough already without the extra jabs, and I could do one of two things: make life worse for people or make life better. And I wanted to do the latter.

"He showed me how to see the good in people. I knew then that, *this* is what I wanted to stand for. And I knew that, if we as a school community joined together—guys and girls, equally—there was a lot of good we could do.

"And make no mistake—I stand behind a lot of what I've inspired this year. I absolutely believe we should eliminate double standards in this town. I believe women and men are equal and should be treated as such. I believe that guys shouldn't abuse their power over girls, and that there shouldn't *be* any power to abuse. I believe that we should be corrected when we misbehave and do better going forward. And that we should all treat each other with decency, with kindness, with love.

"So the point of this is? I'm sorry. I want to do better. I *can* do better. And I hope you'll join me, too."

I turned off the camera.

"Whoo," Christian said. "Got some dust in my eye."

I laughed, then wiped my eyes.

"Yeah, me too."

CHAPTER 33

One week later

When my alarm went off that morning, I felt a huge pit in my stomach. I took an extra-long time showering, drying my hair, putting on makeup. And when I got dressed, I put on the same champagne colored blouse, pencil skirt and booties that I had worn at the New Year's party. Not because, like I'd thought, it made me look like a takes-no-nonsense New Yorker. It was because it was the most appropriate thing I had to wear for court.

Okay, not a legal court exactly. It was Peer Jury. Since what I had done was not a cut-and-dry school infraction—nor could it be proven that I had perpetrated anything on school grounds, I could not technically be punished by the school administration, much to Dean Squared's dismay. Instead, I had to face a seven-member jury of my peers, to see what punishment they'd dole out. Dean Squared had recommended expulsion, and that was on the table.

Christian and I got in the car to head to school at 6:30 that day—because to add insult to injury, the whole thing would take place at 7 AM, and then I had a full school day after this.

"You want me to stick around for this?" he asked.

"No," I said firmly. "No, I'm sure it'll be embarrassing enough without witnesses. And anyway, Dad's got you on powerwashing the driveway today, right?"

"Ugh, don't remind me."

Our parents were appropriately mortified when we both, together, came clean to them about what we'd done. They thought about it for a couple of days and decided to make the punishment fit the crime. Both Christian and I would be doing physical labor—rebuilding the deck, washing the cars, helping refinish the basement, cleaning the house from top to bottom—and get this, earning one point back per chore. Once we got to 100, we'd start getting our privileges back, one by one. Until then, we were both grounded from electronics and the car (well, except Christian was also ordered to drive my ass to school each day, plus he had to get Mom and Dad Starbucks on his way home).

So, I got to the Current Events classroom, where the peer jury would be held, and opened the door. And inside, I found a jury of my nightmares.

Hugh.

Seamus.

Trevor.

Two freshmen—a guy and a girl, but I didn't recognize either one of them.

One sophomore, Grace Childs—not exactly known for her kind nature. And if I was remembering correctly, she was on the cheerleading squad with Kaia. And I definitely recalled that my mom beat out her mom for treasurer of the Snow Ridge Junior Woman's Club last fall. Great.

And, finally, Lindsay.

Also inside, courtesy of the Mock Trial team, was my public defender, Ainsley—who, with any luck, would be my saving grace. I knew her a little, since she was in FEC and in a couple of my APs. I hoped that also meant she could help get me out of this disaster.

"Hi," I whispered.

"Hey, Bethany. I'm gonna be straight with you," she said, right to the point. "This isn't a slam dunk, but I'm gonna do my best. Ready?"

"As I'll ever be," I said with a tight smile.

Lindsay, as president of the Peer Jury, then called the meeting to order.

"Let's start proceedings," she said in a clipped tone. "Prosecution?"

We all looked around the room. The prosecutor hadn't shown up yet.

"Ugh," Lindsay muttered. "We'll give him two minutes to get here. Otherwise, it's a mistrial."

Everyone started to whisper moan about how early it was. Then, the doorknob opened, and in walked Shane, wearing a rumpled suit.

I buried my head on the desk.

"Sorry I'm late," he said, throwing his backpack into a chair. "Ready for opening statements?"

"Yes," Lindsay said with a sigh.

"Great." He pulled a piece of paper from his pocket. "Who you see before you is Bethany Cummings. She has admitted to the heinous crime of bullying. And I have seen it in person. This is not something that should be swept under the rug. She comes from a violent bloodline and should be duly punished."

Good grief. Still driving the bitter bus over that concussion, apparently.

"And," he continued, "it is not enough for her to serve detention. It is not enough for her to serve suspension. Nay, she is a stain on the fabric of Snow Ridge High and deserves to be expelled permanently from this fine institution. I am sure the esteemed members of the jury will agree. Thank you."

He walked back to his desk, avoiding my eyes.

"Defense?" Lindsay asked.

Ainsley stood up, adjusted her skirt, and walked to the podium.

"It's true that Bethany has admitted minor involvement with this silly, juvenile system to keep track of how well boys in this school treated her," she began. "But there is no evidence—none whatsoever—that it was ever conducted on school grounds. Moreover, she was never the instigator of this alleged document. She merely confided in her best friends about this, in effort to share her concern over how they were being mistreated, or dare I say, abused. Perhaps abused by some of the very people in this room?" she added, raising an eyebrow. Seamus rolled his eyes.

"The fact is, Bethany has committed no crime—other than poor taste in guys. If that were a crime, then half the planet would be in jail. Bethany simply cannot, and should not, be unfairly reprimanded. Thank you."

"Okay," said Lindsay. "Evidence from the prosecution?"

"Exhibit A," Shane said smugly, with a printout of the list. "As you'll see here—in Appendix A—it specifically lists Bethany Cummings as the creator of this point system." He blathered on for another minute. I couldn't even listen.

"Defense?" Lindsay said, after he finally sat down.

"I'd like that exhibit to be stricken from the record," Ainsley said. "It's circumstantial evidence."

"It is not!" Shane sputtered.

"It is," Ainsley said evenly. "First of all, it was a Google document that was created by someone other than Bethany—created by an anonymous source, only implicated with initials 'KO.' Second of all, it was a shared document among fifteen people. Any one of them could have said anything in this document, but it doesn't make it true. For example, I could state in a document that Shane McAdams has a micropenis. Would that automatically make it true?" she asked innocently.

Shane turned bright red.

"Order," Lindsay said, rapping her gavel. "Sustained. Character witnesses are next. Prosecution?"

"Um," Shane said, growing more embarrassed by the minute. "I don't have any. Just the formal recommendation from Dean Dean for her expulsion."

What an asshole. When Dean Squared had called my dad in advance to tell him he was suggesting I be expelled, I had never—*never*—heard Dad scream like that before. I was all the way up in my room, and I could hear Dad below yelling on the phone how "you had no right to say anything " and "your little sociopath Seamus has been bullying kids for years," and well, you get the picture. It was safe to say that they were no longer going to be racquetball buddies. I'd never loved my dad as much as I did that day.

"Fine," said Lindsay. "Defense character witnesses?"

I didn't know anything about this. And I had no idea who would even want to show up on my behalf. But before I knew it, Ainsley spoke up.

"Yes," Ainsley said brightly. "The defense first calls Ms. Knox."

And just at that moment, she entered the room.

"Sorry I'm late," she said briskly, moto helmet tucked under her arm. She went straight to the podium and began.

"I'm here as a character witness for Bethany Cummings, and I'm here to assert that throughout the five months that I have known her, Bethany has shown nothing but character."

She looked me in the eye and continued.

"Bethany has fought adversity, malevolence, sexism, and double standards, all in efforts to ensure that her fellow classmates—female and male alike—were treated as equals. She's used her platform to give a voice to those who have been pressured into silence. She's questioned authority when it needed to be questioned. Including the questioning of her own."

My heart swelled at this, and I fought back tears.

"She shows wisdom beyond her years, and that is why I support Bethany Cummings as her character witness."

Lindsay nodded her dismissal, and Ms. Knox left the stand. She tapped my desk and smiled on the way back to a seat, and I mouthed "thank you" as she passed by.

"Anyone else for the defense?" Lindsay asked.

"The defense calls Curtis Snyder," said Ainsley.

I hadn't even seen him come in—he must have snuck in the back when Ms. Knox was talking.

He was in khakis, a button down, and a vest (*swoon!)* and ambled up to the podium like he was a guest star on *Suits*. Again, you practically had to pick my jaw up off the floor.

"I'll make this short," he said, addressing the jury. "Bethany Cummings, like Ms. Knox said, shows true character. When she has found herself lacking, she has gone back to the drawing board on her own self. She makes no excuses for her mistakes, and unlike many, she does not gloss over them. Rather, she seeks to right her wrongs and to never make the same mistake again. I am confident that she did not engage in bullying, nor would she ever intentionally do so. And that is why I support Bethany Cummings as her character witness." He shot me the tiniest of smiles as he concluded.

It was really, really hard to keep the tears back at this point. And then right after he sat back down, my mind was officially blown.

The door suddenly opened, and there was Lana, wearing her 'Don't FEC with us" t-shirt.

Lindsay started to snap, "Peer Jury is in sess--"

"I am responsible for the Snow Ridge Point System," Lana interrupted. "Not Bethany Cummings."

Right after her trailed Sarah, wearing the same t-shirt.

"I am responsible for the Snow Ridge Point System," Sarah echoed. "Not Bethany Cummings."

Next came in Colleen, who was also carrying a "FREE BETHANY" sign.

"I am responsible for the Snow Ridge Point System. Not Bethany Cummings."

And then, one by one, came in all 30 members of FEC, wearing the same shirt. And every one of them, one after the other, said the same thing, louder and louder over the banging of Lindsay's gavel. The last person to come in was Ash.

"I am responsible for the Snow Ridge Point System!" she shouted. "Not Bethany Cummings!"

At this point, tears were completely streaming down my face.

"Order!" Lindsay screamed, her face getting red.

The FEC members finally quieted down, but Lana was the self-appointed spokeswoman.

"You can haul Bethany in here, but the last thing she is guilty of is bullying," Lana said firmly. "And moreover, there is no justice in the fact that one of her jurors is the son of her accuser."

"That's quite a fair point," agreed Ainsley.

With 30 pairs of eyes staring down Seamus Dean, he looked, quite frankly, scared as hell and began to shrink in his seat.

"Again, order!" Lindsay said firmly. "The Peer Jury is not on trial here. Bethany is. Now," she added, shaking out her hair. "Are there closing arguments?"

"The prosecution rests," Shane mumbled.

"So does the defense," Ainsley said proudly.

"Okay. The jury will deliberate next door in the European History classroom and be back once we have reached a decision."

As the Peer Jury members shuffled out of the room, one of the FEC members said under her breath, "We're coming for you next, Seamus." He whipped his head around and darted out the door.

Lana and Ash came to my desk and fiercely hugged me.

"You guys," I said, still crying. "I had no idea."

"No one wanted to see you take the fall for this, Bethany," said Lana. "I mean, expulsion? That's ridiculous. You don't deserve that. And we weren't gonna just sit by and let that happen without a fight."

"No way, no how," Ash agreed. "Ride or die."

I hugged them both again, and then watched as they went back to their seats. Curtis was still in the room, up against the back of the wall. My eyes held his for a long moment, and for a second, it felt like we'd gone back to a simpler time (e.g. April). He looked like he was about to come forward, but then, the door opened, and the jury filed back in, with varying levels of emotion on their faces.

"All rise," Lindsay said.

We did.

"Each member of the jury will state how they find the defendant."

First up was Hugh.

"Guilty," he said, looking right at me with contempt.

Second was the freshman girl I didn't know.

"Not guilty."

Third, Grace Childs.

"Guilty," she said, a smug look on her face.

Fourth, Seamus. Like I even had to guess.

"Guilty."

I did the mental math and realized I was totally screwed. I wondered if could still get in college if I was going to have to get my GED.

Fifth was the freshman boy. I couldn't even look.

"Not guilty."

My ears perked up.

Sixth was Trevor Chen.

"Not guilty."

What?

I looked at him quizzically, and he smiled at me.

But that left Lindsay herself as the seventh vote.

She stood up and cleared her throat. She paused, looking at the FEC members, looking at Curtis, looking at Ms. Knox, and finally looking at me.

"Not guilty."